ONE DAY YOU'LL GO

Sheila Schwartz

SCHOLASTIC BOOK SERVICES

New York Toronto London Auckland Sydney Tokyo

Cover Photo by Owen Brown

ISBN 0-590-31572-2

12 11 10 9 8 7 6 5 4 3 2   1 2 3 4 5 6/8

Printed in the U. S. A.   06

ONE DAY YOU'LL GO

A Wildfire Book

WILDFIRE TITLES

Love Comes to Anne by Lucille S. Warner
I'm Christy by Maud Johnson
That's My Girl by Jill Ross Klevin
Beautiful Girl by Elisabeth Ogilvie
Superflirt by Helen Cavanagh
A Funny Girl Like Me by Jan O'Donnell
Just Sixteen by Terry Morris
Suzy Who? by Winifred Madison
Dreams Can Come True by Jane Claypool
    Miner
I've Got a Crush on You by Carol Stanley
An April Love Story by Caroline B. Cooney
Yours Truly, Love, Janie by Ann Reit
Dance with Me by Winifred Madison
One Day You'll Go by Sheila Schwartz

CHAPTER ONE

It was mid-August, at the beginning of the apple harvest, when the hitchhiker appeared at the Wrights' fruit stand. At another time, Kathy's parents might not so readily have hired him to work there, but during apple harvest season her father needed all the supplemental labor he could get. In addition to the early apples, there were still peaches and pears to pick.

Kathy was working at the stand, stacking the shelves with her mother's homemade jams, jellies, relishes, pickles, pies, and apple butter, when the boy walked in. He looked about seventeen years old and was pale and ragged, his blond hair too long, his blue eyes bloodshot. He walked over to where she stood working; then, seemingly exhausted, threw his knapsack down with a thud and wearily sank down beside it.

"Hey, you," he said to her, "your sign says, 'Free Cider.' Could you get me some? I'm bushed."

To Kathy, this was the final irritant in her wrecked summer. All during vacation, apart from her boyfriend Chuck, who had to work at his family's gas station, all of her friends had taken courses, gone on picnics, and hung out at their favorite swimming hole. But not Kathy. Day after day she had been forced to work here at this boring stand. Well, forced was probably not exactly the right word, but it might just as well have been. In previous years, her father had been able to hire a full-time person to take care of the stand and Kathy had only worked weekends. But not this summer.

Hail had done so much damage to the apples the year before that the Wrights had only just squeaked through the winter. So, there had been no extra money to pay a worker for the fruit stand, and there was no question that Kathy would have to work full-time all summer. They had always been a close family, and her love and appreciation of her parents was shown by her being as cooperative as possible. It would have been inconceivable, like hurting herself, not to help out during a difficult time. Whenever the harvest was disappointing, and that happened more often than she wanted to remember, it was necessary for all of them to pull together. You just couldn't spend your life growing up around apples without understanding the facts of survival.

So she accepted the necessity of spending her precious summer vacation working, but she certainly didn't like it. She felt caged in, never really free, so she was especially resentful when this hitchhiker, who quite evidently was *not* tied to a fruit stand or anything else, just drifted in and asked her to wait on him. He hadn't even said, "Please," and she didn't like the tone of his voice either.

His head pillowed on his knapsack, the boy lit a cigarette and lay there lazily smoking. Mr. Wright hated and feared smoking, not only for health reasons, but because he always worried about fires. That was one of the few rules he insisted on for workers around their orchards and buildings. "No Smoking."

"Hey," the boy called to her again, "didn't you hear me? I asked for some cider. Are you in a service business or not?"

"I'm certainly not in the business of serving free cider," she said coldly. "You can just get it for yourself. See that jug over there? Just help yourself. And take a look at the sign next to the jug. It says only *one* free cup without a purchase. Do you want to buy something?"

"Buy something?" He laughed. "You must be kidding."

"We have the finest produce in the valley,"

she said indignantly. "I'm sure there's something you must want." It was incredible that people might stop in, drink their exceptionally good cider, and then buy nothing. Fortunately, it rarely happened.

"Are you stupid or something?" he demanded. "Can't you tell from looking at me that I'm broke? I haven't had a good meal for days."

Lazily, he stood up and walked over to the jug. Ignoring what she had said, he filled three glasses of cider from the spigot and downed them quickly, one after another. She had stopped working and watched in annoyance as he drank. If he weren't so bad-tempered he'd be pitiful. His blond hair was unkempt, too long; his blue eyes looked red-rimmed with fatigue; his hands were dirty, and she could see that his fingernails were bitten and uneven. His jeans were ragged, his torn sneakers had broken laces, and his T-shirt was dirty and frayed. To complete the unsavory picture, his body was thin.

He threw himself back down on the ground when he had finished drinking. Reluctantly compassionate, she took an early Mac out of a large barrel and handed it to him. He nodded in thanks, immediately bit into it, then lay back and watched her while she made peanut butter. He carefully noted her slight, firm, athletic body, neat in jeans and cotton turtleneck, and her pert face, which combined serious, brown eyes reflecting her basic stability and good sense, with an up-turned nose that seemed to reflect her desire to play and to escape from this eternal labor. Her clear, white skin and reddish-brown ponytail completed a very pretty picture.

"Not bad," he grinned when he had finished his examination. "Not bad at all for a country girl."

He certainly was condescending. "Do you expect people who live in the country to look like pigs or cows?" she asked.

"I certainly didn't expect them to look like little beauties," he said with perfect poise. She flushed. None of the boys she knew in school, and certainly not her boyfriend Chuck, could say something like that without fainting with embarrassment. Embarrassed herself, she couldn't meet his eyes; nobody had ever called her a little beauty before. She turned away to her work.

"Hey," he called. "What's your name?"

"Kathy," she said shortly.

"Chris," he told her. "Greetings. Why don't you sit down, Kathy, and have a little chat. Nobody's watching."

"It doesn't matter if someone's watching or not. I have to finish my work."

"What devotion. What do they pay you an hour, Kathy?" he asked.

"Unfortunately," she said wryly, "*they* do not pay me at all. I am *they*. My family owns these orchards and this stand. I guess you might say I work for my daily bread."

"Cripes." He yawned. "You must be simple. I wouldn't even walk across the street for my mother unless she paid me first. What a sucker! Well, I guess you can get all the apples and cider you can drink."

"That's right," she said curtly. "At least I work for what I eat. I don't go around drinking other people's free cider."

"Oh," he moaned in mock contrition, "I'd write you a check, but I don't have my checkbook with me. Would you like me to fill out an I.O.U.?"

"Actually," she answered brusquely, "what I'd like would be for you to leave me alone so I can go on with my work."

"I'll help you," he said. "I don't have anything else to do or anyplace else to go."

"No, thanks," she said.

"Why not? I'll work off these three monumentally expensive cups of cider."

"You'll make mistakes," she answered haughtily, "and I don't have time to teach you."

"Come on now, love," he said in that insolent, lazy manner, "what kind of intellect or training do you need to stack jelly jars?"

She ignored him and he lay there on the ground, as relaxed as an old dog, while she continued with her work, fumbling, blushing, and self-conscious as she felt his eyes on her, angry that he was forcing her to be aware of his existence. Suddenly, a two-pound jar of grape preserves crashed down to the floor and broke, oozing the sweet-smelling jam and broken glass all over the floor.

"There," she snapped, "see what you made me do?"

"Come on, Kathy, I'll make a deal to help you clean up that mess and to work with you for the rest of the afternoon, if you'll give me dinner and a couple of dollars. What do you say? I assure you that you'll be pleased. You'll beg me to stay."

"I can't make decisions like that. I have to ask my mother or father."

"Of course," he mocked, "like the good little girl you are. I'll go ask your father or mother. Where's the phone?"

"We don't have an extension here," she said. "My mother's up there, at our house." She pointed to their hundred-year-old white frame house that her mother always worried was a fire trap. "Listen, I don't want to hurt your feelings, but there's not a chance my mother will hire you. You don't look very strong. And my Dad always insists that people who work at the stand look super neat."

"Don't judge by what you now see before you," he gave a little bow. "The human body needs daily care. Even all your loveliness would look pretty seedy if you'd been on the road for a week without a good meal or a shower. But I assure you, I'm a real knockout when I'm cleaned up."

"Don't say I didn't warn you," she said.

"Come on." He smiled ingratiatingly. "What do you have to lose? How can you turn away a starving man? Run up to your house and ask your mother. I'll keep an eye on things here." He noted her hesitation.

"Why the reluctance?" he asked. "I'm as honest as they come. You don't have to worry about leaving me here. I'll watch your dinky little stand. Surely you're not concerned that I'm going to abscond with a basket of apples, swill on cider, or debauch with apple butter."

"I can't go," she said firmly.

"Oh, cripes," he moaned. "I'm starving and you're cogitating. You'd be sorry if I dropped dead right in front of you. Listen, Kathy, if it's the cash drawer you're nervous about, you can lock it."

"I'm not supposed to leave the stand," she apologized, embarrassed by his uncanny perceptiveness, "and I'm not going to just because some stranger drops by and asks me to. If you want to apply for a job, you can just go on up to the house and ask my mother yourself. If she says you can work today and stay for dinner, I'll go along with it. But I wouldn't get my hopes up if I were you."

"Don't you worry," he laughed, "I'm always a wow with older ladies. Living with *my* mother has made me an expert."

"I'm not worried in the least," she answered, finding him brash and offensive, "and my mother is not an older lady who would be wowed by you in the slightest. She's the most levelheaded person I know, and she hates rudeness and conceit just as much as I do. I expect she'll give you a piece of apple pie and send you on your way. So, good-bye, and it's been nice meeting you and I don't expect to see you again."

"Wrong," he laughed. "I'm leaving my knapsack here. I suppose I can trust you."

"Very funny," she snapped.

"Bet you a quarter she'll adore me," he laughed. "Back in a jiffy to do my part."

She looked after him in puzzlement as he scampered up to her house like the god Pan. He certainly was a peculiar character, completely unlike any local boy she had ever met. His mind worked differently. It would be impossible for a local boy to even think in terms of charming an older woman. Another strange thing about him was the way he spoke. Perhaps he was from New England. He hardly opened his mouth, and his style of speech seemed simultaneously lazy and insolent, as if he were always making fun of her. It was a kind of different drawl, unlike the speech in upper New York State. Mostly, it was the way he said his "a's" that sounded so foreign. It was the kind of strange speech that would cause him to be teased unmercifully if he went to school here in Huguenot.

She hadn't had the heart to turn him away automatically, but she was relaxed in the knowledge that her mother would handle the situation. Her mother was not only kind, she was perceptive. It wasn't perceptiveness that came from education, but that came from a loving heart. Mary Wright had an emotional ESP that helped her to instantly understand the quality of a person. And she would never hire a stranger who seemed to threaten them.

The family had become increasingly nervous recently about strangers, ever since their friend, the police chief, had warned them about the age of their house. "It's a fire trap," he had said with anxiety. "If it ever starts to burn, get out immediately. It would go instantly; seconds would count."

One day, a friend of the family had been at their house when a truckful of teenagers had driven up, gone down the path to the orchard, and driven off after they had denuded an entire apple tree.

"Aren't you going to stop them or call the police?" the friend had asked her father.

Jack Wright was as sensible as his wife. "If I do, the next time they might just come back and toss a match at the house or orchard. I just figure those apples they're stealing are a kind of fire insurance."

Well, Kathy didn't think Chris was going to burn down their house, but she felt a general uneasiness at his weirdness. She shrugged off her thoughts of him and went back to stacking. Half an hour passed before he came back with her mother at his side. They were both laughing and talking.

"Your mom gave me milk and cookies," Chris said, "and she invited me to dinner. I told you she'd like me. And I like her."

You fake, Kathy thought. He seemed to have fooled her mother. Her father wouldn't have been so gullible, of that she was certain. But he was away. He had gone to a meeting of the local apple growers to discuss a ruling of the Department of Environmental Conservation. The DEC, as the farmers referred to it, had recently banned the use of a pesticide called Endrin, and the Northeast Fruit Council had gone to Albany to protest.

"Where's Mr. Wright?" Chris asked. "I'd like to meet him." Without hesitation, Mrs. Wright told him about the Endrin problem. To Kathy's surprise, Chris seemed really interested. Or perhaps, she thought, he was merely putting on an act to please her mother.

"Does it matter if they ban that stuff, that Endrin?" he asked. "Aren't there lots of pesticides, maybe better ones? Personally, I'm opposed to all pesticides. I don't think they're really necessary, that ecologically they're bad."

Kathy looked at him in exasperation. She'd been through this argument lots of times in school with kids whose families were not involved in agriculture. They just didn't understand. It was even more annoying when customers would stop at the stand, go into raptures about the quality of the apples, then launch into diatribes about the evils of pesticides, without any realization of the fact that without them, they wouldn't be eating fruit of such high quality.

"Honestly," she told Chris, "it just kills me to see people who don't know what they're talking about trying to express opinions. You called me a country girl; You're obviously a city boy. What do city people know about pesticides or agriculture? All they have to do is to go to a fruit store and plunk down their money, and one thing we know for sure, they don't plunk it down for fruit that looks imperfect."

Mrs. Wright broke in mildly to explain. "Endrin is the only effective way we've found to combat the pine voles."

"What are they?" Chris asked.

"Little rodents," she told him with an involuntary shudder. "They're about an inch long and they burrow around the roots of apple trees and during the winter food shortage, they eat the bark from the roots and trunks and cause permanent damage."

"I can see why that's serious," Chris said. "If Endrin is the only thing that does the job, why won't the DEC let you use it?"

"They say that Endrin has a highly toxic character," Mrs. Wright explained. "That it poses a threat to everyone: animals, man, and the environment; that in Virginia, where they've used it for a long time, they've produced Endrin-resistant voles. But they did let the apple growers in this region use it once in 1977, and there didn't seem to be any bad aftereffects at all."

"What will you do if they continue to ban it?" he asked.

"Pray, I guess," she joked. "Now it's time to get to work. Kathy will show you how to bag the apples and peaches. Just watch what she does, Chris. She'll show you the right bags for each, how many to put in a bag, how to close them, and where to stack them. If she doesn't need you for a while, you can help the men in back. We stay open until seven during the summer. If you get hungry, just have some fruit."

"And, Chris," she added tactfully, "do you think you'd like a shower before dinner?"

"I'd love one," he said fervently.

"Fine! Kathy will show you our little apartment above the garage. Past summers our foreman used it, but it's empty right now. Just one other thing. I notice that you smoke. Please don't smoke up there at all. This whole place is a potential tinder box."

"I'll remember," he said. "You don't have to worry."

"See you later, kids. I have to get back to my pies."

"What a lovely lady," Chris said to Kathy as her mother walked away. "You're really lucky."

"Thanks," Kathy snapped. "Now let's get to work."

"Yes, ma'am," and he gave a mock salute.

Why did he seem to go out of his way to annoy her? He didn't seem malicious. Well, maybe he just had a strange sense of humor. Firmly, she began to teach him. First she took him in back of the stand where the men were working.

"The apples come along this grader," she said, "and you sort them according to size into boxes or bags." Then she showed him the three different standard sizes. "I think the first thing you should do is to make some boxes in here. Just fold them in half and staple them with this stapling machine. You'll have to keep sweeping the floor constantly because of the leaves from the apples." She pointed to where the brooms were kept. "When you get 25 boxes finished, just pile them on a skit. I'll work on the bags meanwhile and take care of the customers."

She went back out front to wait on the occasional customer, but during free moments kept peeping behind to watch him. To her surprise, he worked steadily and diligently until it was time to pull closed the heavy wooden doors, padlock them, and turn on the night lights. The workmen went out the back way and closed up there. Then she motioned to Chris and he followed her to the garage. She unlocked the door to the stairs. They climbed them together, and she showed him the shower and where the clean towels were kept.

"Come up to the house as fast as you can," Kathy told him. "It's late enough as it is when we get through eating and start to do the dishes. This week, in addition to everything else, it's my turn to wash."

"Don't you have a dishwasher?" he asked.

She shook her head. "No."

"You're the first family I've ever met that didn't have one," he said. "Why don't you?"

"Oh, for heaven's sake," Kathy said, "you act as if everybody has all the money in the world."

"My mother couldn't exist without a dishwasher," he said.

"She obviously takes better care of dishes than she does of you," she answered, somehow feeling momentarily inferior because they didn't have one.

Chris wasn't offended by her rejoinder. "You're absolutely right about that." He laughed wryly. "She takes better care of most things than she takes care of me."

He certainly was a strange person, she thought again. He said things that were so unexpected; his thinking was different, too.

"Try to hurry," she urged.

Her father was already at home, and Kathy ran to him and gave him a kiss and hug. "What happened?" she asked, knowing the answer just from the expression on his face.

"They just don't want to listen," he said,

momentary depression making him look a lot older than his forty years. "They just don't seem to understand that at two to three thousand dollars an acre, there's no way any farmer, who isn't crazy, is going to spoil the land that's the source of his living. It's technology that's polluting, not us. But farmers have been getting bad publicity and it isn't fair. We get bad press about migrant labor, bad press about chemicals, bad press about spraying. I don't know why, but the reports continue to be slanted against us and the very people who write them probably go out and insist on buying perfect fruit without ever seeing any connection between cause and effect. It's so discouraging, it makes me want to drop it all and buy a motel somewhere in the South."

"You don't mean that," Mrs. Wright broke in. She had heard these threats whenever the problems started to pile up. "You know you love this land. It's been supporting apple growers for the past two hundred years. If your ancestors could manage with all their problems, we can, too."

"I don't know," he said gloomily. "Times have changed. People just weren't as fussy. But now everyone's picky. They want 95 percent fancy, blemish-free fruit, and you know that to make a living we have to produce a thousand bushels an acre." He was as cranky and despondent as Kathy could remember.

"The hell with all of them," Kathy's thirteen-year-old brother Stephan said, bursting into the room. "We'll just go right ahead and use the Endrin and we won't tell them. You and I, Dad, can do it, and they'll never know the difference."

"You can bet they'd find out," Mr. Wright answered. "But even if I were willing to do that, and I'm not, it's no longer possible. They've put a freeze on Endrin. You can't even buy it anymore in New York State, and to tell you the truth I'm concerned they might turn out to be right about the effects of it. Then how would we feel? They had some environmentalists testifying today that it poisons rabbits and deer."

"I wish they'd get rid of all the rabbits," Stephan said. "You should see what they did to our vegetable patch. And there are too many deer anyway. They're just afraid we'll thin down the herds and spoil the hunting season. It's not fair."

"Hypocrites," Kathy added.

"There's nothing to be done," her father sighed. "There's been so much bad publicity, it might hurt sales if people found out we'd used Endrin."

"Time to eat," Mrs. Wright called. She walked into the living room and gently laid a hand on Mr. Wright's shoulder. "I suggest we stop this discussion right now so we don't all end up with indigestion."

Just then, the door opened without a knock

and Chris walked into the room. Kathy noticed that he'd cleaned himself up, changed to a slightly neater T-shirt, and that he looked much better than before.

"And who are you?" Mr. Wright asked coldly, unwilling to confront any new problems in his present mood.

"Chris Landers at your service," Chris answered in the cocky manner that Kathy found so annoying.

"Haven't you heard of knocking?" Mr. Wright snapped. "We were just about to have dinner. What do you want?"

"He's our guest," Mrs. Wright said, stepping in quickly. "I invited him to dinner. He did a fine job helping Kathy at the stand today." As always, Mrs. Wright managed to calm the situation.

"Didn't mean to snap at you, young man," Mr. Wright said, "but I've been up since five this morning and I'm completely exhausted. When I saw you I felt I couldn't deal with another problem. Glad you're not a problem. Let's go eat."

They filed into the dining room, and Mrs. Wright seated Chris next to Stephan. Instantly, Stephan started to chatter away, and Kathy liked the way Chris listened to him and acted as if what he had to say was really important. The family members bent their heads for grace, and out of the corner of her eye Kathy saw Chris light a cigarette and smoke it casually while waiting for grace to be over. Mr. Wright looked up and glared at him in anger.

"One of my main rules around here, young man, is, 'No Smoking.' That means no smoking at any time, anywhere. Is that clear? If you cannot get through dinner without a smoke I feel sorry for you, but you'll have to go down the road, away from the house, to do it. But even if I did permit smoking at ordinary times, I would not permit it during grace. I expect visitors to this house to abide by our rules."

"Sorry about that," Chris said. "I had no idea that it would be of interest to you whether I joined in grace or not. I would assume that's a matter of individual conscience."

"Not in my home it's not," Mr. Wright answered. "What do you do in your own home during grace?"

Chris let out a short bark of a laugh. "In my home," he said, "grace has never once been said since the day I was born, and I'm sure not before then either. My mother would think that saying grace was super square, like a Norman Rockwell drawing. I'm sure she wouldn't believe that people still say it. I mean, she'd be just as amazed that you say grace as you probably are that she doesn't."

Everyone sat there speechless. To ease the tension, Mrs. Wright began to ladle her famous vegetable soup out of the large, white ironstone tureen, which had belonged to her mother and grandmother. Chris looked at the food on their heavy, old, round oak table as if he were admiring a fine painting. In the center was a steaming loaf of Mrs. Wright's homemade dill rye bread. She had cut off a few slices, which lay there invitingly beside the rest of the loaf. In a sparkling glass bowl there was a large spinach salad with little, round cherry tomatoes and sliced white mushrooms.

The family began to eat and pleasantness was restored as Chris raved about Mrs. Wright's cooking. "The best soup I've ever had," he said, enjoying the many fresh vegetables, the big chunks of meat, and Mrs. Wright's famous, secret blend of spices in the soup.

But Mr. Wright was not going to let go that easily. "Is it really true," he asked, "that you never say grace in your home?"

Chris nodded. "I told you, my mother thinks that kind of thing is square, old-fashioned, and out-of-date. Besides that, we never sit down to dinner this way, as a family. Most of the time I was growing up my meal companions were either maids or the TV."

Kathy listened to him suspiciously. It wasn't that it couldn't have been true. But he said all these things so cheerfully, as if he didn't mind at all eating his meals with the TV. Maybe it was all sheer bravado, a valiant effort to mask his feelings of sadness or loneliness. Well, her mother had always told her not to judge too quickly.

"Does your mother cook for you?" Mrs. Wright asked, curious about a woman whose behavior seemed so foreign to her.

"Are you kidding?" Chris laughed. "She can't even make breakfast. Anyway, she never gets up until the afternoon."

Her parents and Stephan were now all watching Chris compassionately. Only Kathy held back and reserved judgment. She looked at him surreptitiously. Cleaned up, smiling, talking animatedly, he looked far better than she would have predicted. Of course, his hair was still too long and she knew that probably bothered her father. But it didn't matter because there wasn't the slightest possibility of Chris's being there past dinner.

Mrs. Wright and Kathy brought out the rest of the dinner from the kitchen: beef stew with onions, carrots, and potatoes.

"The food gets better and better," Chris raved. "Are you a graduate of a cooking school?"

Mrs. Wright told him "no," and beamed at him. Why, she was as fluttery as a young girl! Kathy felt angry at him for flattering her mother. She knew it was all an act; hadn't he told her that he was a wow with older women? But part of her enjoyed seeing her mother's pleasure. They all took her pretty much for granted, Kathy realized guiltily.

"I grow all the vegetables myself," Stephan said. "I'll show you my vegetable garden tomorrow if you like."

"Chris won't be here tomorrow," Kathy said coldly. "He's just passing through."

"Oh, I don't know," Chris said. "My plans are always subject to sudden change."

"You've told us a little about your mother," Mrs. Wright broke in. "Do you have a father?"

"Oh, Mom," Kathy said testily, "why don't you leave him alone. Just because you're feeding him, he doesn't have to tell you his life story, does he? It's the same thing you always do with hitchhikers. Just because you give them a lift, you think they have to talk to you."

Chris ignored her. "My father died when I was a baby," he said, "and my mother has had a total of four husbands."

The family dropped that topic immediately, but Kathy could see the look of dismay her parents exchanged. Her parents had married right out of high school and had lived more happily together than any other couple she knew. In her high school class, many of the kids came from broken homes, but that had never been the slightest possibility for her parents. The very idea of it was outside the realm of their lifestyle. Their major problem was not with each other, but with the fact that they had never made quite enough money to cover their expenses. The idea of having four husbands was as remote to them as would be the idea of marrying a Martian. They were, Kathy thought, looking tenderly at them, wonderfully old-fashioned, loyal, and loving to each other. Life was hard enough for them outside the home; within, they provided comfort for each other.

"Does your mother work?" Mrs. Wright asked. "Or is she a housewife?"

"She neither sows nor does she spin," Chris said. "She has never worked a day in her life at a job and she is certainly not a housewife, if by housewife you mean someone with housewifely skills. No, she neither sows nor spins, but she certainly does reap."

"What about you?" Mr. Wright asked Chris. "Where are you coming from and where are you going?"

"I'm coming from nowhere and I'm probably going nowhere," Chris said.

Again, Kathy's parents exchanged glances. It was the private look they had between them which they reserved for dire subjects, such as sex, atheism, Communism, and cancer. They were good people, but so unsophisticated. Kathy thought they would have fitted in, without difficulty, to small-town, rural American life of a hundred years ago.

They had always lived right here and had never traveled or gone away to college. Before her father owned the orchard, his father and grandfather had owned it, and her mother was a local girl. Early marriage and children had, to Kathy's mind, stuck them forever in this nothing place.

"I don't suppose you'd like to give me a job, would you?" Chris asked Mr. Wright. "You wouldn't have to pay me much if I could have my room and board."

"I don't know," Mr. Wright answered. "You'd have to get a haircut. Why would you suddenly want to work here?"

"Why not," Chris said. "I have one more year of high school, but I don't feel like going back. I've been thinking about looking for a job and then was lucky enough to drop in here. I've never met nicer people. So it just seems like a good resting point to me."

"You haven't been in trouble with the police, have you?" Mr. Wright asked suspiciously.

"Absolutely not," Chris assured him.

"Have you any idea of the work we do here?" Mr. Wright asked. "It's not a resting place."

"I worked all day today," Chris said.

"That's just the tip of the iceberg," Mr. Wright told him. Mrs. Wright had brought in dessert, Apple Brown Betty, which Chris was eating with the same enthusiasm with which he'd devoured the rest of the meal. Poor thing. He must have been hungry for a long time, Kathy thought. They took their mother's superb cooking for granted.

"Is there anything much to do besides picking the apples and putting them in the boxes?" Chris asked. The entire family burst into laughter.

"I'll try briefly to give you some idea of what's involved," Mr. Wright said. "A grower's year follows a definite pattern. In late winter or early spring we do the pruning to keep the trees open and to prevent them from growing too tall. Twelve to fourteen feet is high enough. Then we spread fertilizer around the trees, from the trunk to below the outer branches, so the rain will wash it into the earth to the roots. After that, we have to begin spraying for insects and disease. Flower beds and leaf buds form in late spring and summer, and the next spring the buds burst open. Then come the blossoms, usually during the first two weeks of May.

"That's when we have to worry. One year, a bad hailstorm hit us in May and we produced less than half our usual crop of McIntosh. If nature doesn't work against us, then all summer the apples grow and ripen in the sun. We harvest during late summer, fall, and winter. Our main commercial crop is in late September and October. That's when there's a lot of work to do, young man, and when we need all the help we can get. We pick the apples by hand and I use migrant labor, but I also use local help.

"Now, if you're really interested in a job and want to stay and work with us, I could fit you in. But I couldn't pay you more than minimum wage and I don't really need you for more than a few hours a day. You can start off by continuing to help Kathy, and eventually we could teach you how to pick."

"I don't care what you pay me," Chris said.

"Is he crazy?" Stephan whispered to Kathy.

"There's something else we would have to get straight," Mr. Wright said. "If I hired you, I'd expect you to stay on through the rest of the summer and fall. That's our harvest time. Because if it's just summer work you want, I can get lots of kids around here who are willing to do that. I need someone who's *not* going back to school in September. I wouldn't need you in winter, and, besides, there'd be no place for you to stay. That room over the garage is not insulated. You couldn't stay there once the frost came. You'd have to look elsewhere then; head for your home."

"I'll stay as long as you want me, then take off," Chris said.

Kathy felt she had to say something since she was obviously the only member of her family who hadn't fallen completely under Chris's spell.

"Don't you think we should know a little more about you before giving you a job?" she asked.

"I don't know why you should," he said in that cocky manner that set her teeth on edge. "I'm sure you don't know much more about any of your migrant laborers. How much information is really necessary for me to stack jars of jelly or fill bags with apples?"

Kathy looked at her parents, but they just smiled and said nothing, so she gave a little shrug and gave up for the moment. It had now become their problem; she could not spend her life worrying about her parents.

Later, Kathy and Stephan did the dishes while their parents continued to chat with Chris.

"Isn't that the limit," Kathy complained to her brother. "Just inviting a stranger in that way?"

"You're really getting weird," Stephan said in his characteristically direct way. "You used to be so friendly. I like him. I never met anybody like him before. Mom and Dad like him. Why don't you like him, Kathy?"

"I don't know," she said, not really understanding herself. "It's not exactly that I don't *like* him, it's that I don't trust him. There's something about him that doesn't ring true. His speech is so different, for one thing. Then it's his manner. I mean he's a tramp who acts like a king. That's what's peculiar to me. Maybe he's just escaped from jail or a mental institution. Maybe he's an ax murderer. Remember that spooky movie we saw, where a guy escapes from a mental institution and starts to kill people in his hometown?"

"Sure, but that was a movie," Stephan said. "Things like that don't happen in real life. It was really great talking to him, kind of like having a big brother."

"Do you feel that way about Chuck?" she asked.

"Sure, I like Chuck, too. I don't have to only like one person. Anyway, I've been talking to Chuck for years. Chris is different and he's fun. Chuck is never fun."

Kathy sighed. It was obvious that she was completely outnumbered in her feelings. There was nothing she could do now but to bide her time. And Stephan was right about Chuck. He was solid, reliable, substantial — a known quantity. But never, in all the years she'd known him, had he been any fun.

CHAPTER   TWO

When she and Stephan returned to the living room after finishing the dishes, Chris was talking away to her mother while sitting at her feet and holding a skein of wool, which Mrs. Wright was winding into a ball. Mr. Wright sat in his easy chair reading the evening newspaper, also completely adjusted to this stranger in their midst. She remembered a television movie in which the stranger was an escaped murderer from a mental institution. In the film, when the police were asked, "How could he seem so normal?" a policeman had answered, "This type of schizophrenic always seems normal."

She had to admit that at the moment, Chris seemed almost like a member of the family. She and Stephan plunked themselves down in front of the television, but she kept listening to Chris and her mother talking off to the side. He seemed to know exactly how to please Mrs. Wright, even agreeing with her that the peak of popular music was during the big band era. He was familiar with the music of Glenn Miller and he and her mother eagerly traded Miller favorites.

Her mother sighed. "I've never learned how to do these contemporary dances like the Hustle."

"I'll teach you," Chris said. "I'm a great dancer."

Kathy looked at her mother with curiosity. She had never even thought of the possibility that her mother might like to dance. How strange! In fact, she had never thought her mother desired anything other than staying home and doing exactly what she always did. She felt a little stab of jealousy that her mother should be revealing something to a stranger that she had never shown to her own family.

After the eleven o'clock news, Kathy went with Chris to show him where her mother kept the set of clean sheets and to explain how the electric heater in the room worked. Resentful, inhibited, and ill at ease, she walked silently beside him, not knowing what to say to make conversation.

"Beautiful night," he said, and she nodded her head quickly in agreement.

"I am really bushed," he said. "Can't wait to get into a real bed. I'm never going to understand how anybody can think camping out is fun."

"Didn't you enjoy any of it?" Kathy asked.

"No," he grinned. "I like to look at nature through a picture window. Between the mosquitos and the hard ground, I never slept for more than an hour without waking up. That little room over the garage looks like paradise to me tonight."

They climbed the steps to his room, and Kathy showed him the sheets and electric heater. "I won't need that tonight, of course," he said. "But it's good to know about for those cold mornings later on."

"Are you really going to stay here for a while?" she asked.

"I said I would, didn't I?" he answered. "I usually keep my promises."

"But don't you have to tell your mother where you are?" she asked him. "I mean, if my parents didn't know where I was, it would practically kill them."

"There are parents and parents," he said softly. "I assure you my mother is not the slightest bit worried about me. She knows I'll turn up sometime or other. She's perfectly happy as long as I'm not causing her any trouble.

"I may notify her in a few days," he added in that infuriating lazy drawl. "That is, if I decide she deserves it. I have to think about it."

"I couldn't imagine treating my mother that way," she said.

"Well, little farm girl," he drawled again, "I'm sure there are many things in this big wide world that you couldn't imagine, that aren't dreamt of in your philosophy. But that doesn't mean they don't exist. It strikes me that your experience of life has been extremely limited. I'm certain there are other things besides my treatment of my mother that you couldn't imagine."

She stood there confused, not knowing how to talk to him and resenting him for making her feel so uncomfortable.

"Let's not talk about my mother anymore," he said. "Admit that you're delighted I stayed."

"I certainly am not," she flared up, "and furthermore, don't think I haven't noticed you flattering my mother just because you want to stay here."

"I'm not flattering your mother. I really like her. I've never flattered anybody in my life. Why would I even bother?"

"I just told you," she said, "in order to stay here."

"And why do you think I'd go through any exertions for that?" he asked.

"Because you have no money, no clothes, no place to stay. I think you'd do it to be fed."

"Oh, Kathy," he laughed, "it's not a matter of life or death if I stay here. And I'm not stopping for your mother's cooking, great as it is. I'm treating your mother like the lovely lady she is, which is more than I can say about you, O hostile one."

"I am not hostile," she snapped.

"Did it ever occur to you, little country girl," he said, "that I wanted to stay because of you? I'll never forget that first sight of you stacking jelly jars."

"You're not funny," she said. "I hate to be teased." In fury, she dashed down the stairs, slamming the door behind her.

"I wasn't teasing," he said softly to himself. He made his bed, then lay there smoking for a while before falling asleep.

Kathy ran to her house and burst into her parents' room without knocking.

"What is it," they asked, frightened at her unusual behavior.

"It's that Chris," she stormed, surprisingly close to tears. "I hate him. He's always making fun of me. I don't want him to work with me. It's not fair. You two want to be the Salvation Army and I get stuck with that conceited boy. He's weird and he's always teasing me. How do you know he isn't some kind of crazed criminal or maybe that he's strung out on drugs? You two are so innocent, so naive, you probably never even heard of drugs."

"Of course we have." Her father laughed. "We watch the same TV programs you watch.

I looked at his arms. No needle marks there. He's a nice boy. He was just hungry and we'll fatten him up and see if we can persuade him to get a haircut. You know he's not a crazed criminal, Kathy."

"I don't care," she said. "I don't want him here and I don't want to work with him."

"You really could use some good, daily help," her father said, "and you told me he worked very well today. So why don't you want him here?"

"He took three cups of free cider when he came."

"Oh, Kathy," her mother laughed, "he could bathe in cider and we wouldn't miss it."

"I'm going to have to be nervous about the cash box all the time," Kathy persisted. "I could have had any of my real friends working with me, but you said we couldn't afford any more help. Now you're forcing me to work with a stranger I don't like or trust. Don't I have the right to make decisions like these?"

"Just calm down," her father said. "There are two reasons why we can have him instead of one of your friends, and you know perfectly well what they are. He's working for far less money because of the room and board, which none of your friends need. You know that no local kid would have accepted that. The second reason is that he'll be able to stay and help me when you and your friends begin the fall semester at high school. You should be glad he's here, not angry. It will give you much more freedom."

"No matter what you say," she persisted, "I don't want him. Honestly, I worry about the two of you because you're as innocent as little children. Dad just keeps letting everybody rip him off. People drive up here and steal apples and even your workmen do a lot of goofing off. Dad, you're just an easy mark and Mom is even worse."

Her mother looked at her reflectively. "You like him, Kathy, that's what's bothering you."

"I do not," Kathy said, "and please don't change the subject. You heard what I said about being an easy mark. I bet not another one of my friends' parents would have taken in a stranger this way."

"How did we ever manage to lead our lives before you took charge?" her father asked, more humorously than ironically.

"You managed to lead them very badly," she said, determined for once to express feelings she had had for years. "In one year I'll be graduating, and I want to go away to college. You know that. I have to go away. I'll die or go mad if I don't escape. I want to have adventures, to see new and different places. I want to see the seashore, not only the mountains. But with the marvelous way you two have managed, I don't know how I can accomplish any of the things I want. We don't even have enough money for the family to go to Radio City. I'm the only member of my class who's never been there. When the kids talk about it, I pretend that we went years ago and now I consider that kid stuff. So if we don't even have enough money for the family to make an occasional trip into New York City, how are you going to send me to college? I'll bet you don't even have a thousand dollars in the bank. I'm sick of the way we're always squeezing pennies, so don't talk to me about how well you've managed thus far."

"Have you finished?" her father asked coldly.

"Don't get upset, Jack," her mother said. Then, turning to Kathy, she added, "You really shouldn't worry so much, dear. Everything will work out. I wish you'd try not to get so intense about everything. These little tempests don't change anything and all they do is upset us and make you unhappy."

"Mom, I don't think you heard a word I said," Kathy scolded. "You're so busy making peace all the time, you never hear me."

"Oh, for heaven's sake," her mother said. Now she was exasperated. "I hear you, but there's nothing we can do at midnight except go to sleep."

"And you're still going to let him stay?" Kathy blazed.

"Is that what this scene is about?" Mr. Wright asked.

"No, it isn't," Kathy said. "Everything I've said to you two I've been feeling for a long time."

"I've never seen you quite this way," her mother sighed.

"Then maybe you should start to see me this way," she answered. "I'm growing up and it's time you realized that. I'm almost seventeen, not just your docile little baby anymore. I have goals that go beyond this apple orchard. Apparently this life is enough to make you two happy, but I don't want to live here and I don't want to work here."

"Please, dear," her mother sighed, "let's go to sleep now. There's nothing we can solve tonight. If you want to go away and meet new and different people and have all kinds of new adventures, we'll do our best to help you. But in the meantime, you're here. And today, along came Chris. He's new and different and getting to know him can be as much of an adventure as going someplace new would be. Try adjusting to him. Make believe you've met him in some far-off place."

"You're not very funny," Kathy snapped.

"I'm not trying to be funny," her mother said. "I'm absolutely serious. This is a heaven-sent opportunity for you to meet someone new, and the first thing you want to do is send him away, without any good reason."

"He makes me uncomfortable," Kathy

wailed. "Why can't you put him in the orchards?"

But even as she was asking she knew this was not possible. Very real skills were needed to pick apples, even though people often spoke about pickers as if they had no skills at all. But pickers had to be physically fit, not afraid to handle ladders, not afraid of heights. And they had to understand and appreciate different qualities of fruit. Many of her father's pickers were skilled girls who were excellent, sometimes even a little more careful with the fruit than the men were. It would take a while for Chris to learn those skills. Fruit that was roughly handled was worth less at the market.

"Eventually we will let him help in the orchards," her father said. "We'll train him gradually. Now please go to bed, Kathy. I'm not asking you, I'm telling you."

She went into her room, feeling tired and depressed, and guilty about upsetting her parents. They had enough to cope with without that. Everyone knew how fair and decent her father was. He paid his pickers on a piece-rate basis of forty cents a bushel, and some pickers could pick as many as a hundred and fifty a day. Her father provided transportation, housing, and heat. Sometimes he even provided meals. And he had the best housing, too. His rooms for migrants were clean, with comfortable beds and mattresses, and indoor bathrooms that worked. Inspectors visited the camps at least once a season and they always told her father that his housing was the best.

But, of course, it wasn't only her father's refusal to get rich on the backs of his workers that had caused their problems. This past year, the harvest had been cut in half and that was why the room was empty for Chris to move into. Sudden frost in May had reduced their yield potential, but her father's fixed costs had remained the same. The sudden frost had been one disaster, and then a hailstorm had pitted much of the fruit, so they had to take a lower price for it. Worrying, fretting about the future, not liking herself very much just then, Kathy finally fell asleep.

CHAPTER   THREE

At breakfast the next morning, her father and mother smiled and greeted her as they usually did, and she knew her scene of the previous night had been forgotten. That was the way her parents were, and it was one of the reasons she loved them so much. They taught by indirection, by example.

A few minutes after she began to eat her Wheatena, with their own maple syrup, Chris bounded in, fresh, alert, and enthusiastic.

"Best night's sleep I can remember," he said, "and I'm starved. You'll really see a good worker today." He reached out and gave Mrs. Wright an unself-conscious hug, then slid into a seat and poured himself a large glass of orange juice. He certainly was a fast learner, Kathy thought. He even acted like part of the family now.

"Glad you don't drink apple juice for

breakfast," he joked, as Mrs. Wright gave him a bowl of Wheatena. As they talked, he looked up and listened with unfeigned interest. Kathy hardly paid attention. Apple talk, she thought, always apple talk, and she was as bored with it as Chris was fascinated. One of their friends over near Clintondale had been wiped out by hail. So had another man over by Pancake Hollow. Of course, they could use those apples for cider, but the problem was that salvage apples paid only two to three dollars a bushel instead of the seven or eight dollars that a box of fancy apples would bring. And a lot of growers were increasingly disturbed about the problem of stealing.

"People just stop along the Thruway," her father explained to Chris, "to steal apples. They think that apples grown on trees not too far off the road are public property, there for the taking. They never stop to think that somebody owns those apples, actually needs them for his livelihood.

"We have less stealing than lots of other folks because our house is here, close to the orchards. But people who don't live near their orchards have no way to control the theft. You can't put fences around whole orchards."

"I can't believe there's no way to stop stealing," Chris said.

"Tell you what one friend of mine did," her father chuckled. Kathy sighed. She'd heard this story a dozen times. "One day he drove past his orchard and saw a big, fancy Lincoln Continental parked there. He looked over in his orchard and there he saw an entire family picking. Bold as could be. He could see, even from a distance, that they had already picked over four bushels. So while they were absorbed in their picking, he took the hub caps off their car. He was just sitting there holding them, when the family returned to the car.

" 'Hey, you.' The man from the car yelled at him. 'You've stolen my hub caps. Put them back.'

" 'And you've stolen my apples,' my friend told them. 'If you want your hub caps back, you'll have to pay for those apples.'

" 'Nothing doing,' the man said, 'we picked them ourselves.'

" 'And I picked these hub caps myself, too,' my friend said. They finally exchanged each other's property and the Lincoln Continental went on its way. But my friend knew he had only solved the problem that one time. You can be sure there would be a next time, and a next time, and a next. The landowner has limited rights. You can't throw someone off your property. If you do, you can get sued for liability or personal injury."

"That's one of the most unjust things I've ever heard," Chris protested.

"I could tell you lots more," Mr. Wright said. "Have a nice day, kids." He put on his hat and left for the orchards. Mrs. Wright gave Chris three eggs with country sausages, four slices of homemade bread with their own apple butter, and three cups of coffee.

"If you keep this up," he joked, "I'll be back to my fighting weight in no time. I can't get over the fact that everything is local. Maple syrup from your own trees, eggs and sausage from a nearby farm, and your own apple butter. Best food I've ever eaten."

After breakfast, Chris followed her to the fruit stand and immediately began to work. As the day wore on, she became increasingly pleased with him. He learned faster and was a better worker than anyone her father had hired in the past. He was able to juggle several tasks at one time, didn't mind being interrupted, and was as charming and polite to customers as he had been to her mother. During the day she showed him the peanut butter machine, explained how he could make some in his spare time, and also showed him the different sizes and prices of the apple butter.

"Our eggs are local," she said, "and we carry only the extra large."

During a lull, she took him in back to explain the cider process to him. She showed him how the apples were washed on a conveyor after the electronic control had lifted the crates and dumped them on the conveyor belt.

"A forty-pound box of apples makes 2½ to 3½ gallons of cider, depending on how juicy the apples are. At the beginning of each season, we take apart the press, clean it, then give it an overhauling so it doesn't break down during the busy season. We never pasteurize our cider, just refrigerate it, so it has to be sold and consumed in a week or two."

Chris listened with rapt admiration. "I think you're the most remarkable girl I've ever come across," he told her. "I've never before met a girl who knew so much about how things worked. In fact, I've never met a girl of any age who knew a subject in depth the way you do here."

With a sudden rush of pleasure she realized she was glad he was there. It was only now that she knew how bored and lonely she had been running the stand alone. "I thought you regarded me as just a little country girl," she teased him.

"That, too," he teased back, but it didn't bother her at all. She showed him the rest of the process: The boxes of apples were dumped into the bin and carried through the machine with a water spray across a series of rotary brushes that removed foreign matter from them. Then the conveyor belt carried them to a cutter that reduced them to small pieces. The cut apples were loaded into the hydraulic press that extracted the juice, and the juice was then pumped into a storage tank for bottling.

"We can fill 14,000 plastic bottles at a time," she told him. "The remaining pulp is given away to farmers who use it to feed their cattle and the deer in the area."

After he had been shown everything, during a lull, they stretched out under a tree to relax.

"Enough information for now," he said. "I want to talk about something else."

"What?" she asked.

"You," he said. "There's something I want to know."

"What is it?"

"Do you have a special boyfriend?"

"Sort of," she said with some regret. She had been dating Chuck Diedrich since junior high school and everybody thought it was a big romance, but it was really mainly platonic. They had kissed a few times, but always hurriedly, without much feeling. Chuck was a nice, good boy, kind and respectful, and she really liked him as an occasional friend, but as a boyfriend, he bored her out of her mind. It wasn't that Chuck was dumb. His problem was that he was literal and had absolutely no sense of humor. Seeing him once in a while, say for a football game, would have been all right, but going steady, year after year, would have put a strain even on the wittiest companion.

She had never wanted to go exclusively with one boy, but in their small town, it was difficult to change around. Most of her friends had paired up, as she had, in junior high school, and would marry directly out of high school, just as her own mother had done. Once you were seen with someone, everybody assumed you were each other's property and nobody dared to infringe.

She could have done a lot worse than Chuck. People liked and trusted him, and her girlfriends thought she was lucky. In a way it made life much easier, never having to worry about a date for New Year's Eve or for school dances. But it was all as passionless and predictable as if they had been married for fifty years. It seemed to her that even her parents had more passion between them after years of marriage than she or Chuck would ever feel for each other. She never felt any desire to kiss or touch him, and she was always irritated by his lack of intellect.

But he was so decent that she despised herself for her critical thoughts. It wasn't nice to be so judgmental. That was one of her mother's maxims. Her mother always urged her to look for the positive, and she had to admit that Chuck was cooperative. For example, he would try to show an interest in the things that interested her. If she told him to watch an exciting program on public television or go with her to a foreign movie, he would do it, even though he had little interest outside of sports.

Yes, he was cooperative, he tried, but that wasn't good enough for her. She didn't expect a man to be the leader in a relationship, but she did expect that a couple would, in some way, expand each other's horizons. The sum should be more than its separate parts, but it really wasn't with her and Chuck. She understood even at the age of almost seventeen that this would never be possible between them.

The thing that bothered her the most was Chuck's complete lack of curiosity about people. Once he had told her that he wanted to go camping in Canada for their honeymoon. He had selected a particular place. "The great thing about it," he told her, "is that we wouldn't see another person for the entire time. There wouldn't be another soul for hundreds of miles."

"What's good about that?" she had asked, but all he had done by way of response was to smile back in incomprehension.

Chuck was solid. There had never been any doubt about that. Even in high school he had begun to put money away in his savings account so he could buy a house right after their marriage. The thought of such a house made her shudder. It would be more a prison to her than a home.

With Chuck there would never be any

magic to life. He would graduate from high school with her and would be perfectly content to work either with Mr. Wright in the apple business or at his father's garage, along with his father and many uncles.

"What do you mean, 'sort of'?" Chris asked, breaking into her reverie. "You either do have a special boyfriend or you don't."

"I've been going with someone since junior high school," she explained, "but I don't really want to. We have different tastes. He likes nature and I like people. I don't want to live up here. I want to go and plunk myself right down in the middle of New York City. My special boyfriend, Chuck, that's his name, thinks New York is dirty and crowded and dangerous. He hates cities."

When she'd told Chuck about the extraordinary department stores in New York City, he had asked her what was wrong with the local Sears. When she spoke of famous little movie houses, he said movies came upstate, too, and were a better value at drive-ins. When she longed for New York theater, he said most plays, with the exception of *Grease*, were overpriced and poor value. He said he could see good enough plays on television. When she spoke of the restaurants in New York City, he said there was nothing better than his mother's traditional cooking.

"There's never been anyone I could explain

these things to before," she told Chris. "It's too hard since everyone just assumes that Chuck and I were made for each other."

Chris listened sympathetically without commenting. When she had finished, she asked him, "Do you have a special girlfriend?"

He shook his head. "I've known lots of girls," he said, "ever since junior high school, but at my school it was considered real square to pair up. We just moved in gangs. You might say I've never dated in the traditional sense. So there's nobody special and never anybody as pretty as you."

How warming and pleasant his praise is, she thought.

"Your problem seems quite simple to me," he told her. "If you're not happy going steady with your friend, Chuck, don't."

She burst out laughing. "It's not that simple in a town like this," she explained. "His parents are friends of my parents. In a small town, everybody's connected some way. They go to the same church, to the same library fairs, to the same town meetings. If I reject Chuck, I'm rejecting his whole family network. Besides, my parents really like him. They'd like him for a son."

"But what about you, Kathy? I hope you wouldn't end up with someone just because your folks liked him. What about love?"

"I know," she said, "but I keep hoping,

that is, I've kept hoping I could gradually come to love Chuck. I'll be seventeen in the fall and I'll be graduating from high school next June. Anything could happen by then. Maybe I could get to love him, and then that would be settled. Anyway, I would want to go away to school. The way I've seen it in the movies is that one day you look up and suddenly realize that you've loved someone for years, but just didn't know it. What do you think?"

"I doubt it," he said. "Based on my experience, that spark is either there or it isn't. And if it isn't, right from the beginning, forget it. It never comes."

"How come you're such an authority," she teased, "when you're only seventeen yourself? How did you learn so much about love?"

"Reading," he said, "and watching my mother. I know you and your folks think it's peculiar for someone to have been married four times, but every time my mother married, Kathy, she thought she'd found that spark, that she was really in love."

"It doesn't seem to have worked out very well," Kathy said.

"That's not because she married for love," he said, "it's because she's such an impossible person. No man could hang around her for long under any circumstances, no matter how much of a spark there'd been at the beginning. But even so, she says all the time that love makes the world go round and I think she's right."

He reached across, took her hand in his, pulled it toward him, and gently began to stroke it with his other hand. She could feel her heart pounding right up into her ears, deafening her and dizzying her. Then he took her hand, drew it to his lips, and kissed it. She felt as though her heart would burst. But this is crazy, she told herself, I've only known him for two days.

He took her hand from his lips, turned to her and asked, "Kathy, will you be my special girlfriend from now on?"

It seemed almost as if there were another person inside her who answered him without hesitation.

"Yes," she said immediately. "Oh, yes!"

They sat there smiling at each other until a customer's horn roused them, and they dashed back to work.

Chuck called her that night to discuss their usual Saturday night date and she was consumed with guilt. How could she have told Chris that she'd be his girlfriend? After five years of going with Chuck, suddenly she was proposing to dump him for an itinerant about whom she knew next to nothing and whom she had known for only two days. She decided to clear up the matter the next day, to be firm with Chris. She would not let his charm sway her from what she thought was right.

But she kept putting it off. "I'll tell him by lunchtime," she promised herself the next day.

"I saw deer in the orchard last night," Chris told her as they worked.

"I know," she said. "Isn't it a pain. We don't have to worry about them eating anything right now while there's plenty of food for them, but in winter it's another matter. My dad has found a device that keeps them away from the apple trees and it costs nothing. Can you guess what it is?"

"I don't know," he laughed. "A scarecrow?"

"A variation on scarecrows," she said. "It's human hair. Whenever people buy cider, ask them to bring back the empty plastic bottles if it's convenient for them. We don't pay for them and be sure they understand that we don't use them again for cider. We cut off the tops and fill them with human hair. Nobody knows why it works, but unless they're absolutely desperate for food in the middle of winter, they won't go near the hair."

"I bet they wouldn't stay away from your hair," he said, reaching out and running his hand across her head.

Her heart turned over. How much she liked him. How was she going to tell him that she couldn't be his girl?

"Now, just a little more teaching," she said, "and we'll be through. The prices are marked on the bags of apples, but people can pick their own for half the price. We give them the bags so we can check on the amounts. Don't let them use their own baskets because sometimes the appearances are deceptive and we end up losing a lot of money. It's all right to encourage people to pick their own. It helps us, and a lot of people really like to do it.

"This honey is from our own hives. We sell it in five-pound, two-pound, and one-pound cans. It's cheaper to buy the gallon of cider than the half gallon. Remind people of that. They save thirty cents on the larger one. Over here is stone ground flour that we get from a mill near here. Each of the bags weighs two pounds and we have buckwheat, corn meal, and all-purpose."

She welcomed that morning's rush of customers because it freed her from the necessity to make a decision, and she treated Chris with cold formality until they broke for lunch. They did not close up in case any customers came, but they took their sandwiches and cider onto the small patch of lawn in front of the stand.

"Is something wrong, Kathy?" he asked her after they set out their lunch. "You've been acting so differently from yesterday. Did I do something?"

How could she be cruel to someone who was so appealing? "No," she said, "you didn't do anything. It's me. I said I could be

54

your special girl, but I know that's not possible. After I spoke to Chuck last night, I realized I couldn't do that to him."

"I guess you're right," he said gloomily. "I don't know how long I can be here anyway. I was probably wrong to ask you. But anyway, we can be friends while I'm here. Okay?"

"Okay," she said, wishing he hadn't given up so easily.

That night Kathy's father told her that he would be away that coming weekend. "There's a meeting at Cornell on the subject of Endrin," he told her. "The U.S. Department of the Interior has earmarked 1.3 million dollars in grants to Cornell to find alternative control methods and the growers have asked me to represent them there."

"That's great, Dad," Kathy said. "It's quite an honor. I'm really proud of you."

"The thing is," Mrs. Wright said, "your father wants me to go with him, kind of as a little vacation."

"Wonderful," Stephan broke in. "It's about time you two took some time off."

"I agree," Kathy said. She couldn't remember when her parents had last enjoyed a change like this.

"But," Mrs. Wright went on, "I'm a little anxious about leaving you alone."

"For heaven's sake, Mother, you seem to keep forgetting that I'm going to be seventeen."

"And I'm old enough to stay by myself, too," Stephan said.

"It's just that I'm anxious because Chris is here and you were right, Kathy, we really don't know very much about him."

"No, Mom, I was wrong. I don't think you have to worry at all about our being alone with him."

"Besides," Stephan pointed out, "you'll be seeing Chuck on Saturday night as usual, won't you?"

"Of course," Kathy said evenly.

"All right then," Mrs. Wright said. "I'll cook a turkey and the four of you can have dinner here together on Saturday night." Kathy knew that her parents were reassured by the familiar, dependable presence of Chuck.

Her parents took off at six A.M. on Saturday, and Stephan came to the stand to work with them. At lunchtime, he ran up to the house and brought them a picnic lunch that Mrs. Wright had left, and he kept jabbering away to Chris as they ate.

"Was your mother really married four times?" Stephan asked him. For some reason, this subject seemed to have a strange fascination for him. But Kathy was glad he'd asked because the subject was exotic and exciting to her as well. "Maybe you were only kidding around," Stephan added.

"I wouldn't kid you," Chris said. "How come the subject interests you so much, anyway? Are you planning to have many marriages?"

"I don't plan to have even one," Stephan said. "The only girls I like are Kathy and Mom. How could your mother get four men to like her?"

"It beats me," Chris said. "I'm not only surprised that she got four men to like her, I'm surprised that even one did."

"That's a strange thing to say," Kathy broke in. "Don't you like her, Chris?"

"I do not," he answered, with a little laugh. "She's not particularly likeable. I suppose that in my own way I love her. After all, she is my mother. And I suppose that in her own peculiar way she loves me, too. But she has funny ways of showing it."

"Was your father her first husband?" Kathy asked.

"No, he was number three. He's been dead for fifteen years and there was one other since then. So my mother is almost twenty years older than yours and I think age makes a difference. My mother is impossible. You're lucky to have someone so patient and kind."

Chris was making her think again. First he made her think about Chuck, and now he was showing them how lucky they were to have Mrs. Wright for a mother. Not that they didn't appreciate her. It was just that they probably didn't show their appreciation enough.

"I could hardly believe it when she cooked dinner for us before leaving," Chris said.

"My mom isn't always patient," Stephan said. "Lots of times she yells about my sloppy room or she makes me drink milk, when I don't feel like it."

"That's a good way of being impatient," Chris said, ruffling Stephan's hair.

"Doesn't your mother take care of you at all?" Kathy asked gently.

"No," Chris said. "But the worst thing about her is that she's always having temper fits. She's like a spoiled child. Whenever anything doesn't suit her exactly, she blows up. It's like the geysers at Yellowstone. All of a sudden she goes off and you never know when it's going to happen or what's going to set her off. It really makes me nervous and none of her husbands liked it either. When she's in a bad mood, she just forgets that there are other people in the world who have feelings, too. She has no sense of pride or of embarrassment when she's in a snit; doesn't give a rap who sees or hears her."

Involuntarily, Kathy reached across and took his hand to comfort him. She was glad he would never fully know how much she had disliked him at first.

"Well, anyway," he continued, "when school ended she asked me what I wanted to do for the summer, and I said I just wanted to hang around our apartment, see a few friends, swim at the gym, read, go to the movies, hang out. Well, she started to scream that she wanted me to go cross-country on a teen trip. She was furious that I didn't want to go, but honestly, I get tired of being organized all year. Finally, I realized what she was screaming about. She has a new boyfriend and she wanted me out of the way for the summer. I think she intended to close up the apartment and go to the Hamptons. She acts as if she's doing me a favor to let me live in my own home."

"Is she going to get a fifth husband?" Stephan asked in fascination.

"Who knows?" Chris shrugged.

"You still didn't tell us how you ended up here," Kathy said.

"Fate," he said, looking at her, and she felt her face become warm.

"She went away for a weekend," Chris said, "so I decided to have a big party for my friends from school."

"What's wrong with that?" Kathy said. "I love parties."

"You wouldn't have loved this one," he told her. "A lot of kids got drunk. She came home unexpectedly, right in the middle of the party, and when she saw what was going on, she had one of her fits. Right there, in the middle of the night, she pushed all of my friends out of the apartment. So I grabbed my knapsack and a few clothes and took off.

Trouble is I didn't have much cash. If I had hung around, the next day she would have kissed me, and apologized, and taken me shopping for new clothes. She always figures that as soon as she's ready to make up and be friends, everybody else is, too. And she's always thought she could get me to forgive her by buying me a gift.

"But this time I decided I wasn't going to forgive her so easily. I mean, she really embarrassed me in front of all my friends. I don't know how I can face them. That's why I decided not to go back for senior year. So I sacked out that night with a friend, and the next day I set out hitching. Now you know how destiny led me here."

"Don't you think she might be worried?" Kathy asked.

"No," he closed the subject. "Let's get back to work."

All day Kathy thought about the dinner ahead. She was half-excited and half-afraid. It was exciting to think she would be having dinner with two boys who liked her, but she was apprehensive about the interaction between the two of them. She wondered if Chuck would sense a possible rival and, if so, how he would act. Stolid as he was, he had a bitter temper when aroused.

She found herself wishing she didn't have to have Chuck there at all, but she knew her parents would never have consented to leave

her with Chris without Chuck's presence.
Chuck had slept there many times in
Stephan's room, and he probably would again
that night, although he would have to leave
early to go to church. She, Chris, and Stephan
would work at the stand all day, since Sunday was their busiest day. So it seemed that
she would not have a moment alone with
Chris even though her parents were away.

She left Chris and Stephan at the stand and
went to the house early to get dinner ready.
Stephan had picked some dahlias from the
garden and she placed them in a vase on the
table. Then she warmed up gravy for the
turkey and made a fresh green salad with
big, thick slices of beefsteak tomatoes from
Stephan's vegetable garden. She put a frozen
dill bread and apple pie into the oven while
she steamed their own homegrown corn and
zucchini until it was just tender.

Again, she found herself wishing that
Chuck would evaporate. The very thought of
him depressed her. She remembered that her
high school English teacher had once discussed with the class the concept of psychological time in literature. The teacher had
illustrated the concept by asking the class
how much time passed while the dentist was
drilling on a tooth and how much time passed
when they were having fun. It had been
easy to understand the concept then.

She thought of psychological time now in

regard to Chuck and Chris. She had known Chuck for all of her conscious life and had seen him only a week ago, just before Chris's arrival, but Chuck was as vague in her mind and memory as if he'd never existed at all. For a moment, she could hardly remember his appearance, the color of his hair and eyes. Chris had been there for a short time, but every minute with him was emblazoned in her mind, every detail of his voice and speech and appearance. She felt as though he had been burned into her heart.

She heard Chuck's pickup truck and looked out of the window above the sink, watching him critically as he walked to the front door. He moved like a box on legs, with none of Chris's delicacy. It wasn't that he was fat. Not at all! He was on the high school football team, and even though they never won any games, the boys who played had athletic ability, but he stepped heavily, carrying his body like a heavy burden. He came in without knocking, for he had been an accepted member of the family for many years.

"Hi," he said.

"Hi," she answered.

"Dinner smells good."

"My mom's turkey."

"Need help?"

"No, everything's done."

"I'm bushed."

"Yes," she answered.

"Back to school next week. I don't know how I'm going to do it all: working at the station, football practice, my classes. I'd drop out now but Mom would be upset if I didn't get my diploma. What do you think?"

"You must stay," she said. "It's only one more year, a shame to throw it away at this point. Besides, someday you might decide you want to go to college."

"Not a chance. I'll never sit in a classroom again if I don't have to. Besides, college isn't what I want."

She didn't answer.

"You know that what I want is to marry you and buy a house."

"Don't count on it," she said. "I want to go away to college."

"Maybe you'll change your mind before we graduate," he said. "Just think about it, Kathy. We could have a big family, maybe six kids. I like big families for Christmas and Easter and Thanksgiving. I want two color TV's so I don't have to hassle the programs I want to watch, and I want enough time to hunt and fish and snowmobile. Most of all I want my own house so nobody will bother me about reading or studying or getting good grades. All I want is to be on my own."

She decided that this was the time for action. "Chuck, I have to tell you something and you must believe me. I'm not going to marry you. Not ever. I'm the wrong girl for you. I'd never make you happy."

"I've heard you say that before, Kathy," he said, "but you don't really mean it. You'll come around."

"I do mean it," she said in exasperation. "I want you to start taking out other girls. Please, Chuck. We're not right for each other."

"But you and I get along great."

"No, we don't," she said. "We don't get along now and if we married, you'd be miserable and so would I."

"You'd change once we were married," he said.

"Let's stop talking about it. All right?" she asked.

"All right," he said. He walked over to the table and cut himself a piece of bread.

"Who's the fourth place for?" he asked.

"My dad hired a boy who was hitching through here to work at the stand," she explained, keeping her voice neutral, indifferent. "He's living in the foreman's room over the garage."

"So how come he eats with you?" Chuck asked.

"That was part of the deal," she said, avoiding Chuck's eyes. "He gets room and meals and very, very little pay."

"Why is he willing to do that?" Chuck pursued.

"He isn't happy at home," she explained.

"I thought your dad couldn't afford anyone at the stand," Chuck said.

"I just told you," she said, trying to keep the irritation out of her voice, "that he's working for less than anyone else gets."

"How long will he be here?"

"Until the first frost," Kathy said. "That room isn't heated and the electric heater really doesn't do a good enough job."

"What's he like?" was Chuck's final question.

"He's okay, I guess," Kathy said unemotionally.

Chuck switched on the television, then sank back into her father's easy chair while she went back and forth to the kitchen bringing out the food. He never would have thought of helping in the kitchen. She heard the front door slam and Chris and Stephan walked in.

"The customers really love Chris," Stephan said. "We practically sold out on everything. He talked people into trying things they'd never had before."

"And wait until you see the present I brought, beautiful," Chris called out to her. Neither one of them had yet seen Chuck, sitting in the large easy chair.

Oh, heavens, Kathy thought, I should have warned them. No way out of it now. I'll bet the damage has been done.

"Chuck's here," she called out gaily.

Stephan whirled. "Hiya, Chuckie old thing," he said, pumping Chuck's arm up and down.

He and Chuck had always been good friends. "This is Chris," Stephan added. "Just started to work here."

"Hiya," Chuck said sullenly.

"Greetings," Chris countered. "Nice to meet you. Now, Kathy, here's my present. This is what I hitched into town for yesterday." He held out two bottles of wine that said, "Cabernet Sauvignon Robert Mondavi."

"Should I put them in the refrigerator?" Kathy asked. She didn't want to tell him that her parents had never bought a bottle of wine for dinner. Usually they drank cider; on a rare occasion, beer; and on holidays, scotch. But wine drinking just wasn't one of their patterns.

"Certainly not," Chris said. "We have to open them and let them breathe. I bought this automatic corkscrew just in case you didn't have one."

It was a marvelous metal corkscrew, which fit over the top of the bottle. As Chris turned the handle on it, the curved screw went down into the cork and little arms on the sides went up. After the arms had gone as high as possible, Chris simply pressed down on them and the cork came up.

"Gee, that's super," Stephan raved. "Can I do the second one?"

"You certainly may," Chris said, and he watched while Stephan did it as competently as Chris had. Chuck watched silently, bewildered at an indefinable feeling of exclusion.

"Time to eat," Kathy said.

"If you'll pour the wine, Chuck," Chris said in that cool manner, "I'll help Kathy and carve the turkey. It's one of my special skills."

"No wine for me," Stephan said, pouring the usual cider.

"Eight dollars and forty-nine cents!" Chuck exclaimed, looking at the price tag on each bottle. "I can't believe it. I can't believe anybody would be crazy enough to spend this much money on wine."

"Well, wonders never cease," Chris said ironically as he proceeded to carve with the deftness he had promised.

Kathy was a little perturbed, too, that he had spent so much money. He had probably wanted to impress her and didn't realize she couldn't tell a cheap wine from an expensive one. She hoped he wasn't like certain drifters they employed, who regularly drank up their week's salaries on Saturday night in town bars. It was really stupid for someone who had come to them penniless to show so little respect for money. Chuck certainly would never be so irresponsible.

"I don't know if Kathy's parents are going to like this," Chuck told Chris. "They don't think kids should drink."

"I hardly call this 'drinking,'" Chris said, "but if it bothers you, don't have any. Maybe you would have preferred beer!"

"Hell, no," Chuck said. "My mom's Italian and she serves wine a lot with meals. But you can bet your life she doesn't spend that much. But Kathy's parents don't drink at all."

"Then let's drink," Chris said. He raised his glass. "I propose a toast to the prettiest girl in all of apple land." He saluted her with his glass, then drained it.

"I can't believe you're for real, fella," Chuck said. Then he downed his glass also.

"I don't think she's that pretty," Stephan joked. "But I'll drink a glass of cider to my sister any time."

Thank goodness for Stephan's innocence, she thought, as her brother chatted away during dinner. If not for him, it would have been a sullen, grouchy meal. But eventually Chris's wine helped. At first Chuck sat there stuffing in food while all the time glaring at Chris like a bull warily watching a matador. But after they each had had a few glasses of wine, everybody relaxed.

"I have to do the dishes now," Kathy said after they had enjoyed coffee and apple pie.

"No," Chris said. "Let's finish up the wine first, then we'll all pitch in, Kathy, and do the dishes together."

"I want to watch television," Stephan said.

"A great idea," Chuck said, sounding a little drunk.

Chris started to smoke while they watched TV. "You'd better put that out. You know how my Dad feels," Stephan said.

"He's worried about fires, but with you three here watching me, nothing's going to happen," Chris said.

"What do you think, Kathy?" Stephan asked.

She had never before in her life had so much to drink and she felt very relaxed. It seemed to her that she was having one of the best times of her life.

"Let's not interfere with his pleasure tonight," she told Stephan. "It's such a lovely evening."

"Hey, I think you're a little drunk," Stephan said, "but if you think it's okay, I'll go along with it just for tonight. I guess it doesn't matter if he's careful and Dad doesn't find out about it."

Before they could get to the dishes, it was time for *Saturday Night Live*. Kathy found herself fading in and out as they watched, and before the end of the program, she had fallen sound asleep. She was awakened by Stephan shaking her arm and whispering to her to "wake up quick." She got up and rubbed her eyes. Chris and Chuck were still fast asleep, one on the couch and one in the easy chair. She had fallen asleep in the other easy chair in which she'd been sitting while she watched TV.

"I don't believe it," she said. "It's morning and I never did the dishes."

"Not only that," Stephan said, "but Dad and Mom are outside and they're coming in."

Wearily she sat there, steeling herself for her father's wrath.

CHAPTER   FOUR

"Well," her father said, "what's going on here?"

At the sound of his angry voice, both Chris and Chuck awakened and sat up, looking as dazed and hung over as Kathy.

"What time is it?" Chuck asked anxiously.

"Ten o'clock," Mr. Wright spit out.

"I've got to go," he said. "I've missed church, but I have to get to the station."

"You can go," Mr. Wright said. "I'll get an explanation from these two."

He walked over to the coffee table and picked up the two empty wine bottles, which he proceeded to look pointedly at before dropping them in the waste basket. He retraced his steps to the coffee table where the ash tray held at least ten of Chris's butts. "Smoking," he said, emptying the ashes into the same basket, "despite my strict rule against it."

Mrs. Wright had wandered into the kitchen and came back. "You should see the mess in the kitchen," she complained. "The food has hardened on the plates and pans. It will take hours to get them clean."

"Stephan, you go down to the stand with Chris immediately," Mr. Wright said. "You know how important Sundays are. Kathy, you go in and clean up the kitchen. After the kitchen and dining room are clean, I want to talk to you."

With a sinking heart, she ran upstairs and showered, then spent the next two hours making the kitchen cleaner than it had ever been before. At times, thinking perhaps her father would send Chris away, she found herself close to tears. When she had finished, filled with dread, she went into the living room.

"Sit down," her father said. "Now let us begin. Are you permitted to drink?"

"No," she said.

"Where did the wine come from?"

"Chris brought it as his contribution to the meal."

"Did you ever think to tell him that you were forbidden to drink?"

"I didn't think it would do any harm just this once," she said sullenly. "Chuck's family drinks wine at lots of meals."

"But I'm sure they don't use two bottles for three people. And besides, what Chuck's family does has nothing to do with us." Kathy knew why he hated drinking so much; his father had been an alcoholic.

"And in addition," her father continued, "knowing how dangerous it is to smoke here, you permitted smoking while you three were drunk. Who was smoking?"

"All three of us," she said. She was sorry to put some of the blame on Chuck, but she knew that wouldn't matter eventually.

"I see," he said. "Now suppose someone had fallen asleep drunk, with a lighted cigarette. Where would we be now?"

"But it didn't happen," she said. "Nothing happened, and I cleaned up the kitchen so I wish you'd stop making such a big fuss about what other kids do *all* the time. Honestly, you're beginning to make this house into a concentration camp."

"Now look here, Kathy," her father said. "I would have to be as stupid as you seem to think I am, not to see some connection between these unusual events and Chris's presence here."

She panicked. "That's not true," she said. "It was Chuck who brought the wine, not Chris. It has nothing to do with Chris."

"Don't make things worse by lying, please," her father said. "Chuck never brought a bottle of wine before, not once, so why should he start now? And if he did, it wouldn't be an expensive wine with a French name. Please don't insult me further by lying.

Kathy, I have enough problems as it is and I don't have the energy for this kind of teenage nonsense. If there is any other untoward event, Chris goes. Therefore, if you like his help at the stand, it's up to you to see that he does nothing more to interfere with the workings of this place. Is that clear?"

"Yes," she said.

"All right. Now run along to the stand and send Stephan here. I want to give him a good scolding, too. If he was sober and the three of you were not, it was up to him to make some decisions."

"All right, Dad," she said. "Really, nothing like this will ever happen again. I promise. Tell me how things went at Cornell."

"Not well," he said. "The county cooperative extension agent put our losses in the range of 1.5 to 4.5 million dollars per year alone, due to the pine vole. But the DEC spokesman had the final word," Mr. Wright said wearily, "that Endrin damages the central nervous system of mammals and other creatures, that there's even a likelihood of birth defects in upper level mammals, including man. And if that's true, of course we don't want to use it."

"That finished it," Mrs. Wright added. "That's why we were able to get home so early. They didn't want to hold any more meetings today. We got up at six and had breakfast on the road."

"Oh, Dad," Kathy said, bursting into tears,

"I'm really sorry to have added to your worries. Please forgive me." She ran to him and put her arms around him.

"It's all right." He gently patted her back. "Now run along and get to work. We'll say no more about it."

"Dad wants to see you," she told Stephan. "Then you don't have to come back. You can go off swimming with your friends. Chris and I will be able to manage fine."

"Is he angry?" Stephan asked.

"He was at first," she said, "but everything's all right now. You don't have to worry."

"Looks like I really got you in a lot of trouble," Chris said, "and I'm terribly sorry, Kathy. Do you understand how bad I feel about it?"

"Well," she said, "it was a learning experience. I think Dad will try to forget about it as long as you and I don't do any more drinking or smoking."

"I'll do my best," he said.

"Oh, Chris, I was so frightened for you, for us. I was sure my dad was going to ask you to leave."

"Would you feel bad if I did?" he asked.

"You must know how I would feel. I'd feel terrible. You've turned this boring job and this boring place into fun. I can talk to you better than anyone else in my entire life. I don't know what I'd do if you went away."

"I'm not going away, Kathy, I promise. I'll be here as long as you and your family want me."

He had come out of nowhere and he promised to stay as long as they needed and wanted him. It reminded her a little of the book *Shane*, which she had read in junior high school. She thought of the young boy in the movie calling after him, "Shane, come back." Her eyes filled with tears at the thought of returning to pre-Chris boredom. But he'd promised not to go.

They worked together for the next few hours, hardly talking, not really needing to, just basking in each other's warmth. Here I am, she thought, doing all of the things I've longed so to escape from, and with him at my side it all seems a wonderful adventure. The weather was perfect, her parents had forgiven her, there had been no unpleasant confrontation with Chuck, and business was good. No matter what happens in the future, she told herself, today, this ordinary Sunday in late August, doing what I've always done, this Sunday is the happiest day I have ever known.

At one-thirty, just as they were about to starve, Mrs. Wright came down bringing turkey sandwiches on dill bread with thin-sliced cucumbers and tomatoes inside.

"I'm sorry about last night," Chris said, hugging Mrs. Wright.

"It's all right," she said. "We'll say no more about it."

"How did things go?" he asked her.

"Not well with the Endrin problem," she said, "and now, apparently, deer are becoming another problem. The fruit growers are suffering severe financial losses because of deer. One man who spoke estimated his damage at fifty cents a tree, and another said he had lost ten thousand dollars on both large and small trees. It seems as if the problems never end."

"But it's hard to be sad on such a magnificent day, isn't it?" Chris asked, and laughing, she agreed.

For the rest of the day, Kathy watched Chris with love, taking pleasure in the way he bantered with customers, raced around, and tried as hard to make sales as if he owned the stand himself.

After dinner that night, without even suggesting it to each other, Kathy and Chris wandered out and walked down to the orchards, hand in hand.

"This must be the most wonderful spot in the whole world," he said, holding tightly to her hand.

"When you're not here it's not wonderful. Just lots of back-breaking, hard work."

The moon was full, a beautiful, round, orange, jack o' lantern moon, and her heart felt so full of emotion she thought it would

break. The night was purple and perfumed,
and she felt an excitement and well-being
coursing through her body that left her simultaneously anxious and happy. When Chris
stopped walking and turned to her, gently
tilting her chin up to his, her heart lurched
wildly and she could hardly breathe. How
warm his hand was, how surprisingly familiar. She was filled with a new, strange
sweetness; confused, anxious, wanting to
say or do something, anything, to express
this bewildering rush of tenderness. Then he
leaned down and kissed her. It was a kiss
unlike any she had ever received before; her
first adult kiss. They stood there for a few
minutes in the friendly darkness, clasping
each other tightly.

"We'd better go back," she said at last.
"My parents will worry."

Holding tightly to each other's hands, they
strolled back to the house.

They stopped outside. "I love you, Kathy,"
he said.

"And I love you," she echoed.

"Good night," she whispered, and she fled
into the house and upstairs to her room,
anxious to think about the tumult in her. He
watched her go, then turned and walked
slowly to his own room, stopping for one last,
joyous glimpse of the full moon.

She lay in bed thinking for a while before
falling asleep. It was clear to her that her

major goal for the near future was to see that Chris did nothing for which he could be sent away. But she would have to be very cool about her feelings for him and would have to warn him to do the same. Her parents would be incapable of understanding the storm inside her. Reasonable people can never understand passion. Her parents would have thought the behavior of Romeo and Juliet was excessive, undisciplined, foolish. Her English teacher at the high school had told them that Shakespeare had written them as very young, in order to make their foolish passion more believable and that therefore it was a betrayal of Shakespeare's purposes to have the roles played by older actors and actresses.

But this, she realized with a sudden flash of joy, was exactly what she had always wanted. All this time with Chuck, it had been this kind of emotion she had longed for. Something wonderful and exciting had happened to her at last, and she would do everything possible not to lose it.

She ran down to breakfast the next morning and became euphoric when she saw him at the table.

"Race you," she said, and laughing wildly they zigzagged down to the stand in a tied race. He grabbed her at the end of the race and pulled her to him.

"Are you my girl?" he asked fiercely.

"You know I am," she said, "forever and ever and ever."

He threw back his head and laughed aloud.

There were few customers on a Monday. This was a day to stock up again. One of the men in back had a radio and was playing rock music loudly, so in the middle of their stacking, Chris and Kathy started to dance. They finished the dance and fell into each other's arms laughing, just when Chuck drove up. He sat there for a moment, watching them.

"Hi," Kathy said guiltily, "I thought you were working today."

"It's my day off," he said angrily, "and I drove over because we have some unfinished business from last night. Listen, Kathy, I want to know what's going on with you two. I thought you were my girl. We've been going steady since junior high and you know that I've been saving for a house and everything. I just don't understand how everything got changed around in such a short time. I'm not going to get excited and I'm not going to get in a fight, but I want to understand exactly what's going on."

"I tried to tell you the other night," Kathy said. "We just don't belong together, Chuck. I don't like to hurt you and I always want us to be friends, but in my heart I really never thought I'd marry you. Our tastes are just too different. I've told you that over and over."

"Is it because of him?"

"Chris has nothing to do with it. I'm not planning on marrying him either. After high school, I'm going away to college."

"How long is he going to be here?"

"I told you, until the first frost."

"You're not going to find a boyfriend then," Chuck warned. "You won't have a date for New Year's Eve or the Senior Prom."

"I'll just have to take that chance."

"I still don't understand," Chuck said. "You were okay until he came along. He's mixed up your brains. I tell you, Kathy, easy come, easy go. He'll drift out of your life just the way he drifted into it. Then you'll be left out for the rest of the year, but you won't be able to come running to me. You'll be on your own. There are lots of good fish in the sea, Kathy, and there are lots of girls who would be happy if I even said 'hello' to them."

"Fine," Kathy said. "Is there anything else? Because if there isn't, we both have work to do."

"Okay. You've made your decision, and now you can just plain live with it. See you around."

"What are you thinking?" Chris asked after Chuck had driven off.

"My feelings are mixed," she said. "On the one hand, I really feel bad. Chuck has never been anything but nice and kind to me. But on the other hand, I feel kind of proud of myself. This is the first time I've really had to make a choice in my life. Up until now, everything has run along a smooth, predictable pattern: home, family, school, boyfriend. It scares me, but it makes me feel grown-up."

Later that night, casually, while they were eating, because she knew her parents wouldn't say anything in front of Chris, she told them, "I've broken up with Chuck."

"Oh?" said her mother.

"Why?" Stephan asked. "That was a dumdum thing to do. He was going to let me go camping with him."

"I'm too young to be going steady," Kathy said.

"I see," her father said, looking across at Chris, and Kathy knew they weren't fooled even for a minute.

"Well, dear," her mother said, closing the topic, "it's your decision." And that was all that was said just then.

"I've been thinking about you, Chris," her father said. "I really think you should call your mother. At least tell her where you are."

"I don't want her to know where I am," Chris answered. "The next thing you know she'll come swooping down on us, insulting everybody in her way."

"Really, Chris," Mrs. Wright said, "she can't be as bad as you say."

"She's worse," he said gloomily. Kathy could tell just from his tone of voice that he

was really controlling himself from telling
her parents to mind their own business. She
caught his eye and gave him an imploring
glance, and he understood at once. He nodded imperceptibly back to Kathy, and she
felt pleased that there was someone with
whom she could communicate, almost as if
they had ESP.

"All right," he grudgingly consented. "If
it will make you happy, I'll call her and re-
verse the charges."

He went into the kitchen and Kathy could
hear him speaking, although she could not
make out the words.

"Is everything all right?" Mrs. Wright
asked when he had returned to the dining
room.

"She's away," Chris said shortly. "I left a
message that I'm okay." Kathy could see that
he was bitter and unhappy, arrogant and
cocky again, the way he had been that first
day when the very posture of his body had set
her teeth on edge. "I'd like to be excused
now." Unsmiling, he walked out the front
door.

Kathy ran after him and called, "Do you
want me to walk with you?" But he shook
his head and set off toward the orchard.

"I can't imagine what kind of person his
mother must be to get that poor boy so depressed," Mrs. Wright said. "But now that
he's gone, Kathy, I'd like to know a little
more about this situation with Chuck."

"Count me out," Stephan said, dashing upstairs to his room.

"I've told him many times," Kathy said, "that I would never marry him, that I was going to college. That's still my plan, but today I told him more firmly than ever before."

"Will you two still be friends?"

"I doubt it," Kathy answered, and the subject was dropped. As always, her parents turned the conversation to their work. A friend of theirs in a nearby town had just had the roof of his warehouse torn off by a tornado that had swooped down, but left everything else intact.

Kathy left them and walked out to find Chris. She saw the light in his room, walked up the stairs, and knocked on the door.

"Come in," he called. He was lying on his bed, smoking, and contemplating the ceiling.

"My dad will be furious if he knows you're smoking here!" she told him.

"Tough," he answered. "At the moment, I happen to need a cigarette. Your father's a little paranoid on the subject, Kathy. I'm not two years old, you know."

"I just don't understand you when you get like this. I mean it's like Dr. Jekyll and Mr. Hyde. I can't believe that this morning you were kissing me and asking if I were your girl, and now you're so hostile."

"Sorry. It's that mother of mine. Can you imagine taking off, not leaving word of where she was going, and not even thinking about how I would feel?"

"You did the same thing," Kathy said quietly. "I guess you learned it from her."

He looked at her in bewilderment for a moment, then shook his head in wonder, and let out a little laugh. "So I did. You're right. I acted just the way she does all the time. It's kind of scary, isn't it, that we start to do things ourselves we disapprove of in other people?"

His good humor was completely restored. He sat up, looked at Kathy, and put out his cigarette.

"Listen," she said nervously, "let's go for a walk. You know my parents. I don't think they'd like my being up here with you. Just a short walk because I have to be up so early tomorrow for the school bus. I'll hate being away from you for the entire day, Chris. I wish you'd think about starting school with me tomorrow. I'd introduce you to all the kids and you wouldn't feel left out even for a minute."

"I don't like the idea of being away from you for entire days either," he said, "but school is just out for me for the time being. Maybe I'll change my mind later on."

"Don't you want to go to college?" she asked.

"Not particularly, not right now," he said. "I can always go after a few years if I want to."

"Well, isn't there something you want to be when you grow up?" she asked.

"Who says I'm going to grow up?" he joked. "The reason I have so little interest in going to college, Kathy, is that the things I most like to know and do I can learn elsewhere. I like to travel, to horseback ride, to play tennis. I like to wander in book stores and record stores. I like to go to the theater and movies. I like museums and good restaurants. So why should I want to go to college when all those things exist outside of college?"

"But what about making a living?" she asked.

"At the moment," he said, "I can make as much living as I need working for your family. Later on, I'll get other kinds of jobs. My mother will call one of her friends, maybe at an advertising agency, and I'll be taken on. If I prove myself, I'll be kept on."

"But don't you want to make something of yourself?" she persisted.

"What an old-fashioned expression," he teased her. "What do you mean, make something? What should I make? I am something right now. I don't want to be a doctor, lawyer, or chairman of the board. I don't want to teach, or write, or juggle figures. I just want to listen to music, enjoy life."

"That's a terrible philosophy," Kathy said. "I've seen an awful lot of drifters come through here and they probably all share your feelings, and the result is that they end up at the bottom of society. They drink, have no families, or else have poor, desperate families, and nobody respects them. It's like that Robert Frost poem, 'Death of the Hired Man.' In that poem a poor old farmworker named Silas comes back to die at the home of people who aren't even relatives, just because when he worked for them they were kind to him. When we read that poem in school it gave me the creeps because I've seen so many farmworkers who are just like that. And it's awful for their kids, going from place to place, never settling down to a real home, always feeling like outsiders. I'd hate you to have a future like that."

"Not a chance." He laughed. "Drifting for a while is different from drifting forever. And drifting from choice is also different from necessity."

"But suppose my father took your point of view," she countered. "If he did, there would be no apples grown. And then he wouldn't be able to support his family."

"True," Chris said, "but that's the point, really. He has to support a family, but at the moment I don't have to think about anybody but myself."

What about me? Kathy thought, feeling momentarily let down. This emotion was immediately followed by one of fear. Suddenly she knew with a certainty that came from somewhere down deep within her subconscious, that one day she would wake up to find Chris gone. "Easy come, easy go," Chuck had said.

Just with that one little slip of Chris's, "I don't have to think about anybody but myself," she realized that she was really no part of him, not assimilated into his mind and soul the way he was into hers. But the thought of his going was so painful that she immediately pushed it out of her mind.

The next morning, Chris walked out to the bus stop with Stephan and her. "This is a strange feeling for me," he told her. "For the first time in my life I'm not starting school in the fall along with everybody else."

"It's not too late," she said. "You can get on the bus with us and come and register."

He shook his head. "No, I'd rather stay here. I'll be waiting for you at the end of the day, love."

"Promise?" she asked in a tremulous voice.

"Promise," he repeated. "Are you worried about seeing Chuck?"

"No" — she tried to sound indifferent — "not worried about seeing Chuck. Only worried about not seeing you."

"I'll be here," he said, seeming to understand her concern. "Please don't worry."

"Think about me."

"I can't *stop* thinking about you," he answered. "You've filled up all the empty spaces in my heart and mind."

There he went again, saying all those

wonderful things that any girl would love to
hear, but that no kid around here would ever
dare to say. Funny that words were always
so important. They had read *Cyrano de
Bergerac* in her English class and now she
understood exactly how Roxanne had felt.
Chuck and the boys around here spoke in
monosyllables, but Chris spoke the language
of poetry. He was still standing there looking
after her as the bus pulled away.

"Kathy," her two best girl friends called,
and she made her way back to the same seats
that she, Carol, and Jennifer had been sitting
in since kindergarten. Carol was short,
stocky, and dark-haired, so smart that she
would undoubtedly be the class valedictorian.
Her family was involved in the only other
industry in Huguenot, the state college,
where her father was in the chemistry
department and her mother was assistant to
the Dean of Fine Arts. The kids whose parents were involved with the college were on a
slightly higher social level than those whose
folks worked in agriculture, but Carol didn't
care about that kind of thing. Even though
she was not slim or pretty, she had an assur-
ance about her that Kathy envied. Her model
in life was Margaret Mead, and, as she often
said, Margaret Mead did not look like a
fashion model.

"In fact," she'd once told Kathy, "if an
anthropologist looked like a fashion model,

it would probably hamper research into remote tribes. It would be a handicap for a serious anthropologist to be too beautiful."

Kathy envied her sureness about her goals and values.

Jennifer was at the opposite end of the spectrum from Carol, and the only reason the three of them had become firm friends was because of the years on the school bus. Jennifer's family was one step above migrant labor. Both of her parents drank, and they scratched out a meager living from a little farm. Jennifer was pathetically thin, unhappy-looking, profoundly aware of having been short-changed in life, and anxious only to find a good husband to support her so she could escape from home.

The girls hugged each other and compared notes. Carol had gone on an archaeological dig in Israel with her parents, and Jennifer had stayed home to take care of her younger brothers and sisters. Weekends, she had worked at the local discount store. Kathy waited until the other two had given her all their news, and then she told them her own.

"I've broken up with Chuck," she said in a pleased voice.

"Great," Carol said firmly. "He would have cramped your style for the rest of your life. He was born middle-aged and dull."

"You're crazy," Jennifer said. "He's the greatest boy at school. Could I have him, Kathy?"

Kathy burst out laughing. "He's not mine to give, Jen, but if I could, I'd be glad to."

"I know what," Carol said, "I'll have a party to show our slides of the dig. And I'll call Chuck and ask him to bring you."

A tear ran down Jennifer's face. "You mean you'd do that? Nobody ever did anything that wonderful for me ever before in my life. Wouldn't you be embarrassed?"

"Of course not," Carol said briskly. "Now the question is, who will you bring, Kathy?"

Then Kathy told them all about Chris. "Ooh," Jennifer said, "it's the most romantic story I ever heard. Is he handsome?"

"Gorgeous," Kathy said. "But what about you, Carol?"

"It doesn't matter to me whether I have a date or not," the secure one said. "I might decide to invite a few of the students from the college archaeology society over or the college anthropology society. Or maybe both." Her self-confidence was impressive.

So the party was set for the following Sunday night, and Kathy could hardly wait to get home to tell Chris all about it. She was so anxious that she could hardly concentrate on her classes. She saw Chuck from a distance and waved to him, but he ignored her hand. Then, finally, school was over and she raced home. All the way, her mind was saying over and over, "He'll be gone, he'll be gone." But there he was, leaning up against the mailbox, waiting for her, his blond hair glinting in the sun.

"Wow," Jennifer said, "he is a fox."

"Fine-looking," Carol said, looking at him appraisingly. "I look forward to meeting him at the party."

Kathy stepped off the bus with Stephan. "Hi, Chris," Stephan yelled, and sprinted to the house for his milk and cookies.

Chris reached out his hand to hers and she could have wept for joy. "Hello, love," he said. "I missed you." Hand in hand, their hearts beating hard under the sun of the fine autumn day, they walked in an enchantment of autumn leaves, blue sky, and the warmth of their touching hands. Why does such wonderful happiness make me want to cry? Kathy thought, tremulous and open and loving.

That night her father was going to a meeting of New York State Apple Growers to decide what to do about a sudden oversupply of apples that had resulted in dwindling prices. "You'd think the population explosion could give us ample markets for the apples," he grumbled. "The problem really is transportation. Chris, if only man could find a source of fuel other than oil or coal, or if only we could develop strains of apples that were resistant to fungus and insects, you'd see a golden age of apples."

"Oh, Dad," Kathy said, "Chris isn't interested in all these details about apples."

"You're wrong, Kathy," Chris said soberly. "I'm very much interested. In fact, I've never been more interested in anything in my life. Maybe if I ever decide to finish high school and go to college, I could work on these problems."

"It's a noble career," her father said. "One of my regrets is that I never went to college to study agriculture. I figured I could just do things the way my ancestors did them. But I could have made a greater contribution if I'd been educated. This way, all I can do is grow apples."

"There's no greater contribution than that as far as I can see," Chris told him loyally.

Kathy looked at Chris's face and listened to her father. Would Chris never cease to surprise her? He had no sooner finished telling her that he had no ambitions in life than he was talking seriously to her father about an agricultural career. She felt as if they had all been enchanted since Chris's arrival. He made the mundane seem so interesting. Perhaps she, too, should start to think about going into the agriculture field. Why had she never thought about it before? Probably because she'd always been so anxious to escape to the big city. But living in Huguenot did not have to be imprisonment. That was the way her parents lived because of economic problems, but it seemed to her that she could live a different and better way even if she remained here. In high school she had always been as good in the sciences as in the humanities. And yet she had never before considered going into a scientific field. Why shouldn't she? It certainly seemed natural enough. In her mind she pictured herself and Chris working and experimenting side by side, kind of like the Curies who had discovered radium.

Chris was a catalyst. Never before had she heard her father talk about his educational regrets. Chris's very presence was shaking all the old ways; her relationship with Chuck, her parents, and her own purpose in life. Why, she wondered, had she always thought it was better to teach than to work with apples? With some shame she understood that this was the way she had been rejecting what her parents were and further rejecting the endless problems that were an inescapable part of the agricultural life.

CHAPTER   FIVE

"I have a big surprise planned for your father," Chris told her as he walked her to the school bus the next day. "Just watch the trees on your way home from school today."

At the end of the day, when they reached the beginning of the long road that led out of town and toward their home, Stephan grabbed her arm and let out a yelp of excitement. She looked at where he was pointing and saw the surprise Chris had mentioned.

"When Dad sees this he's going to be pretty mad," Stephan told her, and with a nervous giggle she had to agree. Large signs had been tacked to every tree on the road, and the signs said:

1) Wright apples. We stop spraying four to six weeks before picking time. Buy at Wright's. Route 32.

2) Wright apples. The Food and Drug people certify *OUR* apples pure. Buy at Wright's. Route 32.

3) You'll never be poisoned by OUR apples. Buy at Wright's. Route 32.

4) *Wright's* stand has been certified outstanding by the Building Inspector, the Tax Department, the Health Department, and the Labor Department. Buy at Wright's. Route 32.

"The signs are ridiculous," Kathy said. "Everybody knows that the Food and Drug people stop at *every* orchard to see if there's too much poison on the apples. Everybody's apples are certified. Nobody sprays in bloom."

Apparently, Mr. Wright did not learn about the signs until late afternoon, and it was when Chris walked in for dinner that the full hurricane of his anger was unleashed.

"And whose idea was it," he shouted, "to put those ridiculous signs up without my permission?"

"It was mine, sir," Chris said.

"But he discussed it with me," Kathy lied, "and I told him I thought it would be all right, that you'd be pleased with our initiative."

"Pleased?" Mr. Wright continued to scold, "Do you know what you two may have done? In one day you may have wrecked the spirit of cooperation that we have all struggled so hard to build in this valley." He stomped out to the truck and stomped back in with one sign he had taken down. It said: "You'll never be poisoned by OUR apples."

"What's wrong with that?" Kathy asked nervously.

"I'm surprised I should even have to explain that to you," her father snapped. "You know perfectly well that the sign implies that other apples *will* poison. That's not what we want people to think. We want them to understand and to believe that there are no apples sold anywhere that could poison them. We don't want to even put the idea in people's minds that apples could poison them. But it's not just what customers will think. I'm humiliated at the thought of what my fellow growers will think."

"I don't think anybody will be offended by the sign," Chris said.

"You know nothing at all about our operation here, so your opinion is meaningless."

"But everybody around here likes and trusts you, Dad," Kathy said.

"And I want them to keep right on feeling that way," her father added. "They may think I was involved in this foolish advertising scheme. What you don't know, Chris, is that sales are not our problem. Product is. Our enemy is not each other, but natural causes that diminish our crops. We don't have to compete the way businessmen do. Our only way to survive is through cooperation."

"I only wanted to help." Chris was downcast.

"That's not the kind of help we need up here. Maybe that's appropriate help for the cities, but not for the country. Once we start to compete instead of communicate, we're done for. We learn from each other, help each other.

"Chris, although you've only been here for a little while, you've been fitting in quite well. The family likes you. But you work here, and nothing else. The next time you cause a problem, I'll have to let you go. Is this clear to you?"

"Yes, sir," Chris said.

"Fine. Now I want the three of you to go down now in the truck and remove every one of those signs. Kathy will drive."

"I have a license, sir," Chris said.

"Kathy will drive," Mr. Wright repeated.

"Yes, sir," Chris repeated, but Kathy could tell that under his ritualized, polite response he was angry. He said nothing, however, merely stomped to the truck, held the door for Kathy, closed it for her, then walked around to the other side and sat beside Stephan.

"I think it was really nice of you to try to help," Stephan said. "All you were trying to do was to get us more business."

"He's wrong, you know." Chris was tight-lipped. "But it's his problem, not mine. I'm only passing through. I don't know why I even bothered."

Kathy said nothing, but worked quickly along with the two of them to cover her anxiety. He had said aloud what she feared so terribly. "I'm only passing through."

After they had finished, they sat in the truck for a few minutes before returning, so Chris could smoke a cigarette.

"Are you still angry?" Stephan asked, to break the tension.

"A little," Chris admitted.

"Because you spent a lot of money on the signs?" Stephan asked. Chris shook his head.

"I know why," Kathy said. "You thought he was ungrateful. That's it, isn't it? He really isn't, Chris. He understands, but he's just harried by all his problems."

"I kind of wanted to act as if I were part of the family." Chris said, and Kathy could see that these were difficult words for him to say. "You two are so lucky to have a father. Maybe the best thing for me to do now would be to take off."

Kathy's heart missed a beat. "Please don't be foolish, Chris." She tried to sound cool, not frantic. "Everything will blow over."

"Yeah, stick around," Stephan said. "I really like you. We can make believe you're my brother."

Finally, Chris smiled, and harmony was restored. Then Kathy told him about the party Saturday night to introduce Chuck to Jennifer.

"Are you really sure you want to take me there?" Chris asked, troubled again. "I suddenly have the feeling that I'm messing up things for everyone."

"It will work out fine," Kathy said. "Jennifer will be much better for Chuck than I would be. She wants exactly the same things he does. It really would be a match made in heaven. And Chris, I'm terribly excited about going with you. I'll be so proud to introduce you to everyone. There's not a kid around here who's anything like you."

"Well," he said grudgingly, "let's hope that nothing else goes wrong and that I'm still here for the party."

Kathy lay awake for hours that night, worrying about those words of his. Once, in the high school library, she had come across a novel called *Of Human Bondage*, and the book had scared and fascinated her, almost like a warning about what she was now going through. The book was about a man named Philip, a painter, who was obsessed with a worthless woman named Mildred. No matter what he did, he couldn't get her out of his mind and she, of course, never really felt the same love he did. Kathy was convinced that Chris's feelings for her were not nearly as intense as hers were for him. She still remembered the lines from the novel that had stirred her so much. "He was not happy with her, but he was unhappy away from her. He wanted to sit by her side and look at her."

That was the way she felt about Chris. She was so completely involved with this beautiful stranger that when she was away from him at school she could think of nothing else. She worried terribly about his moods. One day when she came home from school, he gloomily told her that he had been introduced to picking that day.

"How did you like it?" Kathy asked, expecting an enthusiastic response.

"I didn't," Chris said shortly. "It's boring, no fun at all. I had this romantic notion of how great it would be to work with my hands, but it isn't romantic at all. It's just hard and tiring and boring."

"But it has to be done," Kathy said briskly. "If picking was so great to do, you wouldn't have the poorest people in society doing it. That's why my dad tries so hard to make their lives a little better."

Apples were still picked the same way they had been picked for hundreds of years. The picker had to break off the apple stems with quick twists, but not pull the stem out of the apple because this would make the apple rot. At the same time, the picker had to make sure that the spur to which the apple was attached was not pulled off the tree because it would be needed for future growing.

Pickers placed the apples gently in canvas-lined metal buckets, which weighed about thirty pounds when full. But that wasn't the hardest part, because the picker was still on the ground. The problem was getting the higher apples on stepladders. Handling these stepladders was especially difficult because they had to be moved from tree to tree in an upright position. There was an awful lot to think about until a picker became experienced.

Kathy thought to herself, Here it comes. Now he's going to leave. Chuck's mocking words, "Easy come, easy go," suddenly started to roll around in her mind.

"I don't mind picking," Stephan said. "I'll go out with you on Saturday, Chris, when I'm not at school, and I'll show you how really easy it is, once you get the hang of it."

Dear Stephan, Kathy thought. How very much like her mother he was, almost as if he had been born sunny and tactful.

She had never before known so much anxiety. Before Chris, she had been like a child, secure, comfortable, expecting everything to be tomorrow as it had been yesterday and today. But now there was no certainty. For the first time, teachers were commenting at her inattentiveness. Her homework assignments were shoddily done, and she passed through the school days in a dream. Her moods hung on his. When he was gloomy, she was fearful, and when he was cheerful, the warmth and radiance of his smile made her giddy, joyous.

All week, she and her friends talked of nothing but the party.

"I invited Chuck," Carol said.

"I hope you didn't tell him it was for me." Jennifer seemed very concerned.

"My dear girl," Carol said, "don't be so gauche. Boys are not beings from other planets to whom we have to lie. Of course I told him that I was inviting him for you."

Jennifer was amazed. "What did he say?"

"He was pleased," Carol said, "as I expected him to be. After all, his ego has hardly been expanded by Kathy's dropping him for Chris. So when I told him you were extremely interested in meeting him, he was glad. I told him that he didn't have to pick you up, but that if you and he liked each other, he could take you home."

"What does gauche mean?" Jennifer asked Kathy after Carol had left them.

"I don't know either," Kathy giggled, "but I bet Chris does."

"I'd give anything to be as self-confident as Carol," Jennifer said.

"I would, too," Kathy answered. I am going to make a decided effort to be a little more composed, she promised herself. Carol would never waste endless energy as she was now doing. Carol's byword was "self-control," and Kathy vowed she was going to make a greater effort from that point on. When she'd wanted to qualify for cheerleader, she'd gone on a rigid diet. If she could do that, stay away from what was not good for her to eat, she should be able to get these feelings for Chris under control. Loving somebody so wildly, who might not be there one day when she got home from school, was just letting herself in for trouble.

She was almost relieved when Carol's party was put off for a while, because gradually life with Chris was becoming routinized. If he's just here for one month, Kathy told herself, I'll never worry again. And miracle of miracles, the month passed without incident. Chris was always there when she reached home at the end of the day. Evenings with him were especially joyous, for he helped with her homework, with the dishes, and each evening during that glorious Indian summer he took long walks with her. They talked incessantly; Kathy had never felt so at ease, so close to anyone. As she relaxed, her grades started to climb again, her sleeping habits returned to the old patterns, and a thousand times a day she would pinch herself, find she wasn't dreaming, and feel a flash of joy at the goodness of life.

Weekends, they worked happily together at the stand, not even needing to talk. By the end of the weekends they would sell out the cider and the Early McIntosh, which had begun to ripen in August. Some Saturday nights they took Stephan to the town movies, but more often they would just watch television and fall into bed exhausted.

She had been completely lulled into contentment by the time she and Stephan left for school on the Monday before Carol's party. It was shortly after lunchtime when she heard the terrifying announcement on the loudspeaker. "Kathy and Stephan Wright, report to the office immediately. Kathy and Stephan Wright, report immediately." Her heart started to pound, and she raced down the hall, almost colliding with Stephan who was coming from the other wing. They ran into the principal's office and found their mother there.

"Mom," Kathy cried. "What is it? What's wrong?"

"Is it Dad?" Stephan screamed in terror.

"Is it Chris?" Kathy asked through numb lips.

"No, no," she said, "they're all right. You two look as if you'd seen ghosts. They're both fine. Just sit down and I'll tell you why I'm here."

There had been a fire and Mrs. Wright wanted to tell them about it before they heard it from some other kids at school and became frightened. She asked the secretary if they could be excused from school for the rest of the day, and after they were in the car and driving toward home, she told them what had happened.

Shortly after noon, in a period of only twenty minutes, their cider mill and solar-heated storage building had burned to the ground. This was the only genuine solar building in the area; it had originally been built as a poultry house, and then Mr. Wright had converted it to use for the storage of orchard machinery.

"What was burned, Mom?" Stephan asked.

"Everything in the building was destroyed," she answered, for once not the least bit cheerful. "A truck grader, three tractors, and a sprayer. I'm afraid it's going to be a major financial disaster for us, but fortunately no one was badly hurt. I think we have to keep that in mind. We have to be grateful for that."

"What do you mean, 'badly' hurt?" Kathy asked, sensing there was something Mrs. Wright had not yet told them.

"Is it Dad?" Stephan whispered anxiously.

"No, Dad is absolutely fine."

"Something happened to Chris, didn't it," Kathy whispered, filled with terrible fear.

"Yes, something has happened," Mrs. Wright said, "but it's nothing serious. Chris was slightly burned, just his hands. The doctor has already been to the house and bandaged his hands. He doesn't think they'll even be scarred."

"How did it happen?" Kathy asked. Why on earth was she whispering, she wondered. Probably because she was so frightened.

"Chris is really a hero," her mother said. "I wouldn't be at all surprised if the fire department gives him some kind of award."

"Will you please tell me what happened?" Kathy was almost frozen with fear.

"You know that gas tank that was inside the storage building near the door?" Mrs. Wright asked. It was full, and we were terrified that the fire would reach it and it would explode. If that had happened, we might be homeless today, too. The firemen came almost immediately, but the building was already burning out of control. We told them about the gas tank, but nobody dared to go near it. They just kept telling us all to stand back. Suddenly, Chris darted out of reach of their arms, dashed inside the building's door, grabbed the chains attached to the tank, and pulled it outside to safety. We all cheered when we saw what he had done. He burned his hands pulling it out, but he really saved the house and stand for us.

"Kathy, it was a lucky day for us when we hired him. The gas that was still in the tank is no good now because there's water mixed with it. The gas man is coming to drain it and refill it, and then we're going to move it temporarily into the shade of the sycamore tree."

"Drive faster, Mom," Kathy pleaded. Then she started to cry. "Are you sure he's all right?"

"He's fine by now," Mrs. Wright said. "We put him on the living room couch and the doctor gave him a shot, so he'll probably sleep through the night. He has painkillers, and the doctor said he'll be fine in a day or two. I don't think you should wake him up, Kathy. It seems to me that he's in shock. Tomorrow we can move him into Stephan's room for a night or two."

"I won't wake him," Kathy said. "I just have to see him."

"You can trust me though," her mother said. "I haven't minimized his injuries at all. It could have been so much worse. Really, he could have been killed. We're very, very lucky."

"Do they know what started the fire?" Stephan asked.

"Not yet," his mother answered. "But maybe they'll be able to figure it out in a few days."

"How's Dad taking it?" Kathy asked.

"He's pretty depressed," her mother answered. "You can't imagine how quickly the fire consumed the building. Now all our farm machinery is gone and there will probably be no cider this season. It's a terrible loss and the three of us will have to keep cheering your father up."

"Don't we have insurance?" Stephan asked.

"Yes, some," Mrs. Wright said, "but not nearly enough. I guess nobody ever carries enough for replacement. We'll have to get another loan, I suppose. Still, every time I think of what would have happened in this dry weather if the gas tank had gone up, I think we have to count our blessings. The firemen had to water the roof of the apple cooler building anyway to keep the fire from spreading, and immediately after Chris pulled out the tank, they had to throw a wet blanket over it. I think the only way we can survive this is to keep reminding each other how much worse everything might have been."

The trip home seemed to take forever. The moment they reached the house, Kathy jumped out of the car, then remembered to gently open the door to the house. She tiptoed into the living room to where Chris lay sleeping on the couch. Her father sat slumped in his large easy chair, looking old and exhausted. All of his fire and energy seemed gone.

Kathy and Stephan ran to him and hugged him. Kathy began to cry, then Stephan joined in, and Mr. Wright looked as if he would like to join them. But after a while, his traditional strength asserted itself.

"No more tears," he said. "These things

happen. All that matters is human life, everything else can be replaced. Somehow we'll manage. I've already called Pete LeBlanc at the bank and he promised me another loan to replace the machinery not covered by insurance. We have to keep looking at the doughnut and not at the hole. I'm grateful that the cooler wasn't touched and that the harvest will still be all right. We're not desperate. We're not out on the street. I know what you're thinking, Kathy. That I'm going to let you down about college. I don't want you to think that. Somehow we'll manage. You have my solemn word that you'll be able to have your heart's desire."

Now Kathy wept more than ever, touched that in the midst of such catastrophe her father should be aware of her needs. Chris let out a little moan in his sleep.

"That's quite a boy," Mr. Wright said, looking with affection at the sleeping body. "It was a fortunate day when he came to us. I'm feeling a little guilty that I was so hard on him about those signs. He was only trying to do something to benefit us and I scolded him as if he was an enemy. I'm going to apologize to him when he gets up and tell him that I should have been gentler and more appreciative. He's a fine young man, Kathy, and I'm going to invite him to stay with us during the winter, even when we no longer need him to work."

"Great," Stephan said. "He could share my room. I'd really like that. I've always wanted a brother. I mean, in addition to a sister, Kathy."

"When he wakes up," Mr. Wright continued, "I'm going to suggest to him that he go back to school with you and just work weekends, to earn his keep. He doesn't have to drift around any longer or go back to that mother he doesn't seem to care much for. If he wants to stay with us, he can have a permanent home here. He's earned it today."

How can I be so happy in the midst of disaster, Kathy thought. Now I know that at least he'll stay for the year. Her mind started to spin all kinds of future scenarios. Chris going to college with her, marrying Chris at apple blossom time, celebrating Christmas with Chris. She was so filled with joy, she thought she might explode. Chris groaned again, and she went and kneeled down beside the couch. Then she gently soothed his hot forehead with her cool hand. It briefly awakened him.

"Water," he croaked. She held his head up with one hand and with the other she tenderly held the glass to his lips. He took a few sips, then fell back exhausted. His eyes were still open.

"Are you in pain?" Kathy whispered lovingly to him.

He shook his head.

"You're a hero," Kathy whispered to him. "We're all so proud of you."

He looked at her without blinking. Then a tear rolled down his face. He closed his eyes and fell back to sleep.

Kathy stayed home from school the next day to be with Chris. Mrs. Wright insisted that he remain on the living room couch so that he could watch television. Kathy brought him large, wonderful meals, the same meals that he had loved so much when he'd first arrived, but he wouldn't eat. He wouldn't eat and he wouldn't talk; just lay there glumly, focusing either on the television set or on nothing.

"Why is he acting so peculiar?" Kathy asked her mother, out in the kitchen. "He's like a zombie."

"Give him time," her mother said. "He's probably still in shock. We have no way of knowing how long it takes to get over something like this. I also think the painkillers the doctor gave him for his hands must interfere with his functioning. We have to let him get as much sleep as possible and let time be the healer."

"But he seems terribly depressed, Mom."

"Kathy, dear, you're beginning to depress *me*. There's nothing to be done, so either sit there and keep him company and relax about his condition, or else go to school. I'll drive you over now if you wish."

"Okay, okay," Kathy said. For the next few hours, Kathy sat near Chris, knitting while he watched television. He seemed unaware of what programs he was glued to, and he and Kathy did not exchange even a word. At three o'clock, when she heard the front door open, she looked up expecting to see Stephan. He was there; but he wasn't alone. Chuck, Carol, and Jennifer crowded into the room behind him.

"Chuck drove us all here from school," Stephan informed them.

Mrs. Wright came into the living room and greeted the guests with pleasure. "Just in time for some hot, fresh Apple Brown Betty," she said. Carol and Jennifer went out to the kitchen to help Mrs. Wright carry everything in, and Chuck sat down on a chair next to Chris's couch. For a few seconds, Chuck seemed to be floundering for words, then he began to speak.

"Listen, Chris," he said, "I think it was real great what you did here. Everybody in school was talking about it today and all the kids want to meet you. I was, I got to admit it, real sore about you and Kathy, but not anymore. I got to admit that you're a super kind of guy. Honest, I don't think I would of had your guts. They say that gas tank could have blown any minute. Listen, Chris, let's be friends."

"You're being too nice," Chris murmured,

white-faced, unsmiling. "Thank you very much."

"What's wrong with him?" Chuck asked Kathy.

"He's in shock," she whispered. "He's just not as responsive as a normal person would be."

Carol and Jennifer came in, wheeling the tea table with cider, milk, hot Apple Brown Betty, and vanilla ice cream.

"I always say you have the best food in town in this house," Carol said. "You never get this kind of good home cooking from professors."

"You don't get it from alcoholics either," Jennifer said gloomily. Somehow, this last remark struck them all as terribly funny and they laughed, reveling in the release from tension.

Then they looked over at Chris. "He's crying," Carol whispered. "Oh, for heaven's sake, Jennifer, don't stare at him. How gauche can you get? Poor fellow, he probably thinks he's still in the trenches."

"What trenches?" Chuck asked.

"What are you talking about?" Jennifer demanded of Carol.

They really were meant for each other, Kathy thought in amusement. Not one sense of humor between the two of them.

Carol plunked herself down on a chair at

Chris's side, to observe him as a budding anthropologist would.

"Would you mind telling me what you're feeling?" Carol asked Chris.

"Buzz off," he answered.

"How would you describe your emotions right now?" Carol asked with that armor of cheerfulness.

"I wish you'd leave me alone," he said.

"Well," she said firmly, "if you are capable of saying that, I don't think we have any long-range worries about you. I'd like to come over tomorrow and interview you. Perhaps you'll be feeling better by then. I always think it's interesting to catch survivors off guard."

Chris sat there in silence and Kathy could see that he was getting angry. Maybe that's a good thing, she thought. At least he's beginning to react again.

"You just have to be in shape for my party Saturday night," Carol said. "My parents have a film on South Africa, which they want to show at the party. Nothing like a captive audience."

"That sounds dull," Chuck said. "I'd rather dance than see a film about South Africans."

"I agree completely," Jennifer said. "I can't see the point in getting depressed about situations over which we have no control. I mean, why torture ourselves? I see enough human misery in my home every day, not to want to go to the movies to see it."

Carol grinned across at Kathy. "Made in heaven."

"Hey, let's play Scrabble," Stephan said.

"I've got to get to work," Chuck said. "See you all at the party Saturday night."

Stephan, Carol, Jennifer, and Kathy sat on the floor playing, while Chris remained immobile and withdrawn on the couch. After a while, they all gave up trying to talk to him.

"How about everybody staying for dinner?" Mrs. Wright said, just as they were finishing their game.

"I'm not certain that would be right given the extra work," Carol said.

"I'd love to stay and get some good food for a change," Jennifer said.

"Please, both of you stay," Mrs. Wright insisted. "Having guests is good for us. It distracts us from what lies immediately ahead. Why don't you come out and get trays and carry them into the living room, so Kathy can help Chris eat?" But Chris refused to eat and even Carol's persistence didn't bring about any animation.

"Do you think we should call your mother, Chris?" Mrs. Wright asked.

"She's traveling," Chris answered. "I don't think you could reach her. I'll get in touch with her myself when she gets back."

The phone kept ringing for the rest of the day and evening with calls from various people, anxious to meet or congratulate the hero. Chris flatly refused to see anyone, most especially the reporter from the local newspaper. Kathy and Mrs. Wright kept promising callers that they would get back to them as soon as Chris was stronger.

"He'll come around at the party Saturday night," Carol told Kathy before they finally left that night. "It's going to be a memorable one. Every kid in the senior class has been invited on condition that they chip in for refreshments and a gift for Chris. Don't tell him. We want it to be a surprise."

"That's the nicest thing I ever heard of," Kathy said, giving her friend a hug. "I hope he feels well enough to come and I hope the gift doesn't bowl him over. What is it? You can tell me. You know I never talk."

"We had a plaque ordered specially for him that says: 'Hero, Chris Landers, Huguenot, September, 1980,' but that's not the main gift. The main gift is that we've collected over two hundred dollars to go toward the rebuilding of the cider press, and we're going to give it to your family through Chris. I know that's not much money, Kathy, but we simply couldn't get another cent out of these local paupers. Most of them spend more for bowling each week than they contributed, but I'm trying not to look at the motes in peoples' eyes so I have to be grateful for whatever we did get."

Kathy went to the kitchen and told her mother as soon as the girls had gone. Mrs. Wright was as pleased and touched as Kathy had been. "With everything," her mother said, "we're really lucky people." Kathy threw her arms around her mother, and the two women stood there for a moment, hugging each other tightly.

CHAPTER SIX

By Saturday, the doctor had reduced the bandages on Chris's hands and had taken him off the painkillers. Although Chris said his hands no longer bothered him, he still seemed nervous and abstracted before they left for the party. Carol had invited Stephan because of the gift, and also because she was the one person Kathy knew who mixed up all different ages at her parties.

Stephan had offered to help Chris dress, but he said he could manage and apparently he had been able to do so. He had returned that morning to the room over the garage, despite Mrs. Wright's suggestion that he stay at the house until he was completely healed. At seven, they were ready to go.

"My, you three look spiffy," Mrs. Wright beamed. "I just know you'll have a marvelous time. Don't overdo it, Chris. Kathy, you take good care of him."

"I hope this isn't going to tire you too much," Kathy said.

"If it does," he said, "I'll tell you and we can leave."

The party was held in an empty barn on Carol's property, and Kathy could hear the blare of the phonograph as they approached. Apparently, the kids had been waiting for them and when they entered, they all applauded for Chris. He stood there looking frail and embarrassed until one of the girls grabbed him gently by the elbows, careful not to touch his hands, and pulled him onto the dance floor. Kathy was pleased to see that Chris was gradually beginning to react to the music, to dance and smile. Someone brought him a beer, which he downed, and then he continued to dance. Kathy wasn't worried about that. She knew that on this night, many girls would want to dance with him. Carol walked over to stand beside her.

"Thank God he's acting human again," Kathy said. "I was beginning to worry that he might be permanently damaged."

"He looks fine," Carol said cheerfully. "Look at Chuck and Jennifer. They're really having fun together."

Kathy looked and for just an instant felt a pang, but she was still sure she hadn't made a mistake. Just because he was happy with Jennifer, it didn't mean they could ever have been happy together. She had to admit that when she wasn't involved with Chuck, he didn't seem as boring.

The rest of the evening passed in a pleasant haze. Girl after girl asked Chris to dance and Kathy held back, glad to have others take on the job of cheering him up. Finally, at midnight, Carol turned off the record player and pulled Chris and Kathy to the front of the room. Everyone got very quiet as Carol spoke:

"The Senior Class presents this to you, Chris," she said, "in gratitude for what you have done for our very good friends and neighbors. We applaud your selflessness. Further, in honor of you, we now present this check to you to help the Wrights rebuild. We realize that it is only a token, but we wanted to symbolize our empathy and compassion."

Then she leaned over and gave Chris a brief peck on the cheek and all of the other young people applauded. Kathy felt tears stinging her eyes and she gripped Stephan's hand tightly. These were her friends, this was her world, and she felt full of the giving and taking of love.

"We'd appreciate it if you'd open the package, Chris," Carol said briskly, "so that everyone can see it."

Stephan rushed forward. "His hands still hurt," he explained as he proceeded to open the package for Chris and hand the plaque to him.

"Read it, please," Carol said. Chris simply held it awkwardly, looking close to tears.

"I'll read it," Stephan said. " 'In gratitude,' " he read, " 'to Chris Landers for exceptional heroism.' " Tears flowed from Chris's eyes as he turned to Kathy. She ran to his side, hugged him, and gave him a kiss, while the others applauded.

Finally, Chris became more composed, and in a cracking voice he said, "I really don't deserve this." The crowd roared its disagreement, cheered, applauded, and then rushed to eat and dance again.

"Would you like to get some fresh air?" Kathy asked him, and he nodded gratefully. "How do you feel?" she asked after they had breathed deeply of the crisp fall air. He was silent.

"Chris, why are you so quiet?" Kathy asked. "Why are you being so cold to me? I saw you dancing and laughing with the other girls. Why are you treating them better than you treat me? What have I done? I thought we really cared about each other, but you won't even talk to me. Please tell me what's going on."

"You really are incredible," he said savagely to her. She reeled back as if he had physically struck her. "Can't you ever stop thinking about yourself? Ever get out of your skin? Is it impossible for you to see that you have nothing to do right now with what's going on inside of me? I was laughing and dancing with those other girls because with them I could wear a social mask. And in addition, they don't bother me about love. I'm feeling a lot of mental pain right now and there's no room for you in there."

"I care about you," she said softly, holding back her tears. "I want to help you."

"The best way you can help me right now is to leave me alone," he told her. "Now if you don't mind, I'd like to go home. I'm feeling tired."

"Sure," she said, "I'll just go and tell Stephan. Stephan was not ready to leave and said he'd get a lift home with Chuck. So Kathy drove and Chris said not one word to her all the way home.

"Would you like something to eat before you go to bed?" Kathy asked, treating Chris like a mental patient or sick child. "Is there anything I can do for you? Would you like to take a walk?"

"No," he said gloomily, "there's nothing you can do for me. But, Kathy, for what it's worth, I really do care about you, more than anyone else in my entire life."

She stood there crying as he walked away from her, a thin, lonely, depressed figure. She longed to run after him. But if he wanted to be alone, if he still needed time to recover, she would just have to repress her own feelings.

She went to her room, took a long, hot, oil

bath, tried to read for a while in bed, and finally fell into a troubled, dream-filled sleep full of fire and anger. She awakened at six o'clock, checked the time, then slept for another hour. The stand would be open through October on weekends, but she did not have to get down there until ten.

At seven she awakened again, dressed, straightened her room, and finally, feeling depression like a palpable weight on her back, she went down to the dining room. Stephan and Chris were apparently still asleep, but her parents were drinking coffee together companionably. They had found the check, which Chris had asked her to leave for them, on the breakfast table, and both were touched and pleased.

"We certainly are lucky people," her mother said. "So many lonely people in the world, and we live among friends."

"That's right," her father added. "Chris tells me that his mother has plenty of money, but is never happy. She has no roots, no base, just kind of knocks around the world whenever she pleases."

Then Kathy told them about Chris's peculiar behavior. "He's just not the person he was," she said. "I don't like this Chris. I want the old one to come back."

"Give it time," her mother urged.

"I think I'll just stroll down and have a talk with him before breakfast," Kathy's father said. "Maybe I can help. One of the things that boy lacks is a strong father figure."

Kathy and Mrs. Wright were still sitting at the breakfast table talking when Mr. Wright returned. One look at his face told Kathy that something was seriously wrong.

"What's the matter, Dad?" she asked nervously.

"Chris is gone," her father said heavily. "He took his knapsack. The only thing he seems to have left behind was his plaque for heroism. There was no note, nothing at all."

"Oh, Kathy," her mother said compassionately. Kathy just put her head down on the table and wept. Mrs. Wright put her arms around her, and let her cry until she was exhausted.

"I know how much you cared about him," her mother said.

"I must have done something wrong," she wept. "Maybe Chris sensed that I never really trusted him, never really believed in him, much as I wanted to. I read somewhere once that when we're terribly afraid of something happening, we subconsciously do things to *make* it happen. I was so worried every day about losing him that I could hardly breathe on the way home from school. Several times I asked him if he ever would take off without telling me. Maybe that's what drove him away. Perhaps I shouldn't have taken him to the party."

"It's not your fault, Kathy," her mother said. "Why, darling, just try to think how absurd your reasoning is. Chris has done what we know he's done before; taken off. You know he left his mother this same way and he told us she often did the same to him. Try to see how silly it is for you to blame yourself for something wrong Chris did. Nobody could have been better to him than we were. Kathy, it has nothing to do with you. There was always something a little strange about Chris, always a part of him that was unknowable."

"But he asked me to be his girl, Mom," Kathy cried. "I thought that meant something. Why would he say it if he didn't mean it?"

"People say many things they either don't mean or mean only for the moment. There's really no way to deal with it or prevent it. All we can do is to accept the fact, so it doesn't destroy us when it happens."

"I loved him," Kathy said, struggling now for composure. "He was the first boy I've ever loved, and I thought that it would be forever and ever, the way it is with you and Dad."

"Someday you'll find somebody with whom you can have that kind of relationship. Maybe when you go away to college." Her mother brushed the hair back from Kathy's wet face. "Loving Chris, had he stayed, might even have kept you from the right man. It might help you to look at it that way."

"I don't think any way I look at it will be of much help," Kathy said ruefully.

"No, I guess you're right. It will take time."

"Don't you feel defrauded at all, Mom? You were so good to him."

"Whatever debt he may have had to us, and mind you, Kathy, I never viewed him in that way, he repaid us by saving the oil tank. No, I think it was fair exchange. I enjoyed having him here. He left owing us nothing."

"But couldn't he at least have left a note?"

"Perhaps he couldn't think of the words," her mother said. "Suppose he had written, 'I'm leaving.' Would that have been better?"

"Yes," Kathy said. "Somehow I think it would have been better. I would have liked him to show some reluctance, some regret, to have given us some idea that he had liked us. Anything."

"I'm sure he felt all of that," her mother said. "I'm sure that it was all very hard for him. If it hadn't been, he would have faced us and said good-bye. No, I'm certain he can't feel good about this and I'm also certain that some day in the future you'll hear from him and he'll try to explain."

Stephan had come in while they talked and he took Kathy's hand in his own. He said nothing, just sat there holding his sister's hand, trying to make his own warmth and love for her flow from his hand to hers.

"I don't know how I'll go to school to-morrow," Kathy said. "I'll be so embarrassed to face all those kids and tell them Chris went off. Chuck will be especially gratified."

"Chuck's not a cruel boy," Mrs. Wright said, "but in this case, I suggest you tell everybody a little white lie. It will hurt no-body, but it will save you from embarrass-ment. Let's just tell everybody that Chris has gone into the city to see his family doc-tor. What do you say to that?"

"Sure," Stephan said. "I promise that's what I'll say, Kathy."

"What do you feel about it?" her mother asked.

"Grateful," Kathy said soberly. "I feel grateful that I have you two and Dad. I don't feel alone, even though Chris has hurt me terribly."

So it was decided; that was the story they told and everybody accepted it. After all, why shouldn't they? Most people really didn't care, and Chuck and Jennifer were happily involved. But Kathy told the truth to Carol.

"He must have been more traumatized than we realized," Carol said. "He'll be back. And when he returns, what will you do?"

"I'll lock him in his room," Kathy giggled, "and keep him with me forever and ever."

"Don't be so sure," Carol said. "He may not even interest you when you see him next."

"He will always interest me," Kathy said. And that was the end of the discussion.

After that, seemingly, life resumed its normal patterns. All through the fall, after school, she and Carol went horseback riding at the stable across from the high school. An awkwardness had developed between her and Jennifer. "She probably feels a little guilty now about Chuck," Carol said, "but I wouldn't worry about it. She's so involved with him now that I hardly see her myself anymore."

Weekends, Kathy helped at the stand until they closed for the winter. She was grateful for Carol's independence, for they often went to the same Saturday night group parties that Chuck and Jennifer were at, but Carol's caustic, witty presence kept Kathy from feeling lonely. Most of the boys in their class were taken, but neither girl had any interest in the remaining unattached few. For the first time in her life, she didn't mind going to parties without an escort. This is good discipline for me, she told herself, the best kind of preparation for going away to college.

Everybody assumed she had forgotten Chris, but the truth was that she went through her daily routines like an automaton. She laughed and smiled and talked on cue, gossiped, did her homework, complained about her teachers, ate, slept, and worked, and all the while she hid the fact that she felt bereft, bewildered, unresolved in terms of Chris. The truth was that she was waiting.

The week before Thanksgiving the letter finally came. It was a normal day; no warning at all that she would again be suddenly pierced by lightning. Trying to restrain her trembling, she fled to her room with the letter. Then, contrary to her usual fashion, she locked the door, propped up her pillows behind her on the bed, held the letter for a few seconds, then took a deep breath before plunging into the icy water, and opened the letter. With a shiver, she started to read:

Dearest Kathy:

There is no way that I can explain my behavior to you in a letter; no way that I can show you the pain of the period since I left.

I went back to my boarding school, but I will be home for the Thanksgiving weekend. I wonder if you could come into New York City early on Saturday morning. You could stay over through Sunday or return Saturday night, if you prefer that.

We could have a full day on Saturday and do some of the things you've always longed for, such as Radio City. I would also like to show you the Metropolitan Museum, the Museum of Modern Art, and take you to dinner at the Rainbow Room.

My mother, of course, will be here, so you will have the dubious pleasure of meeting her. But I want your folks to know that we would have some form of adult supervision.

Whether you can come or not, and even though I probably do not deserve it, I would appreciate it if you would answer this letter, to the above address.

Please give your folks and Stephan and the kids who were so nice my best regards.

Love,
Chris

She read the letter over several times, feeling a tornado of emotion sweeping over her, remembering the magnificent Indian summer nights when they had walked, remembering his kisses, the warmth of his sudden smile, the pulse that beat in his throat, the way she had moved in an exhilarated daze after their first kiss. She saw his finely chiseled profile, the intense blue of his eyes, the grace of his slender, agile body. She tried without success to feel resentment about the terrible hurt of his leaving and her depression when the agony had dulled to pain. Her own feelings had to be thought through before she spoke to her parents, and after a tortured hour, she realized that there was simply no reason to even weigh the ambivalence of the situation. She wanted to see him, had to see him, if only to put her aborted relationship with him to rest. If she didn't, she felt that for the rest of her life she would yearn for this evanescent, phantom lover.

When she felt she could rationally handle her desire to do as he wished, she looked in the mirror to make certain she appeared composed and calm rather than hysterical or deranged, and walked downstairs to talk to her parents. Her father was sipping cider at the kitchen table, talking to her mother while she made dinner preparations. Without saying anything, Kathy put the letter down in front of him. He read it, but withheld comment while Mrs. Wright read it.

"Sit down, Kathy," she said calmly. "All right, dear, what are your feelings about this letter?"

"Throw it in the fire," Mr. Wright said angrily. "I can't forbid you to go, Kathy, and I wouldn't want this to be my decision even if I could lock you in your room. But

what you are doing is setting yourself up
to be hurt again. It will cost you twenty
dollars round trip, you will spend the day
with him, return here while he goes back to
his school, and for the rest of the year, you'll
be mooning around, depressed and critical
of yourself, because you haven't heard from
him. Then, just as you're getting settled
again, you'll hear from him and the same
thing will happen again. I say that the wisest
thing you can do is to throw the letter away
and pretend it never came. He doesn't even
deserve a response from you."

"Now I'd like to speak," Mrs. Wright said
firmly. "I understand exactly how you feel.
But Kathy has to go. She has to have the opportunity to understand why he acted as he
did. If she doesn't, this will nag at her for the
rest of her life."

"But how do we know," Mr. Wright said,
"that he won't hurt her again?"

Mrs. Wright said quietly, "You can't control the universe. Kathy, you tell us, what do
you want to do?"

"You're right, Mom," she said, "I have to
go. I have to see him again, if only to say
good-bye."

Mr. Wright heaved a gigantic sigh and
capitulated. "All right," he said. "You can
take the 6:55 A.M. bus in and arrange for
him to meet you at nine. I'll expect you to
take the 9:30 bus back that night and I'll

be waiting for it. I don't want you to stay
there overnight."

"If anything interferes," her mother said,
"you must call us immediately."

"Nothing should interfere," Mr. Wright
said.

"Don't worry," Kathy said, "I'll be on that
9:30."

She couldn't wait to tell Carol the next
day. "How does this letter sound?" she asked
her.

> Dear Chris:
>
> I will be on the 6:55 A.M. bus, arriving at
> 9:30 A.M. I will meet you at the bus exit
> into the terminal. I have to take the 9:30
> bus back that evening. It will be very nice
> to see you.
>
> Sincerely,
> Kathy

"What do you think?" she asked Carol
again.

"Pretty frosty," Carol said, "but just
about what he deserves. That's a very fancy
address. He must be super rich. Call me the
minute you get home that night, no matter
how late it is."

Kathy found herself as unsettled in school
that week as when Chris had first appeared.
She kept trying to reason herself out of her

nervousness, but she was afraid she wouldn't look pretty enough for him. Despite the fact that he'd seen her under many hardly glamorous circumstances—sweating as she lifted bags of apples, pushing back her hair when the humidity was high, wearing the oldest sort of work clothes—she still worried.

She alternated between exhilaration and depression. At times this trip to New York seemed so quixotic, so purposeless, so foolish. Her father was probably right, the most sensible one. As usual, her mother understood what she was going through.

"How about going to Sears?" Her mother said one evening. "I think it's time for you to have some new clothes. Nothing like new clothes to give a woman confidence."

"We really can't afford it," Kathy said, for they were all still feeling the terrible pinch occasioned by the fire.

"We'll manage," her mother reassured her. "Even if you're as pretty as you are, new clothes help."

They finished dinner early, then drove to Sears where she bought a tweed blazer, corduroy jeans, a corduroy skirt, new boots, a shoulder strap imitation leather bag, and a green knit turtleneck sweater.

"Oh, Mom," Kathy said, delighted by her reflection in the three-way mirror, "I'll never forget this."

"Ha, ha," Stephan, who had been waiting

for them, teased. "Not until the next time you need clothes."

On Friday afternoon she used a conditioner on her hair, set it in rollers, used a facial mask, and clumsily put nail polish on her fingers and toes.

"I don't know why you're fussing so much," Stephan said. "Chris saw you a million times looking messy, and I never saw him when he didn't look like an unmade bed."

"Don't get me more nervous than I already am," she told him.

"I don't know what you're nervous about," Stephan said. "It's only Chris. It isn't some stranger. Want me to go with you?"

Tempted for a moment, she finally shook her head, determined not to hide behind her brother. "I have to do this for myself," she told him gratefully.

The next morning, Mr. Wright drove Kathy to the early bus. She carried Chris's plaque, a bag of Northern Spys for Chris, and an apple pie and Brown Betty for his mother. Mrs. Wright had managed to make a neat parcel of them, and Kathy wasn't worried about carrying the things because Chris would be meeting her at the bus. In her new shoulder strap bag she had a round trip ticket and a ten dollar bill that her father had insisted she carry.

"I don't need so much," she had told him.

"I would be uncomfortable all day," he

said, "thinking you might be wandering around New York City without enough money." She hugged him hard. At that moment, ten dollars to him was like a hundred dollars to most people.

The sky was gray and winter was almost upon them. She could feel the nip in the air. All of the October apples had been picked: the Cortlands, Red and Golden Delicious, Rome Beauties, and Idareds. They were still picking the last of the Northern Spys, the November apples that were her favorites. As soon as she was seated she picked one out of the bag and bit into its tender flesh. The juice oozed through her teeth and the rich, tart flavor filled her mouth, rose up into her nostrils, and gave her courage. She was glad her mother had suggested that she take these gifts. It might make Chris's mother like her.

The bus ride seemed to take forever. She had taken two paperback books with her, but she was far too excited to read. Fantasies kept tumbling through her mind. Chris wouldn't be there. They wouldn't recognize each other. The bus would be late and he would leave without waiting for her. He would be mugged on his way to find her and she would never know. Perspiring with anxiety she found herself alternately regretting the trip and worrying about whether or not she looked nice enough. At last she drifted off to sleep and awakened only when the driver's voice loudly boomed, "Port Authority Terminal. Last stop."

Clutching her parcels, she walked through the swinging glass doors and instantly saw Chris. She was so astonished at his appearance that she put her packages down with a thud and stood there staring at him in amazement as he darted forward to meet her. Dressed in a navy wool blazer, gray flannel trousers, a blue button-down shirt, striped tie, and glossy black boots, he looked like the ultimate preppy. His spare frame provided a perfect base for the fine clothes, and Kathy found his elegance intimidating. Little as she knew about the world of fashion, it was evident to her that there was a world of difference between his kind of clothing and her new Sears clothes. But before she had a chance to feel more intimidated, he had taken her in his arms and was warmly hugging her and kissing her cheek.

"I can't believe you're finally here," he said joyously. "You look just great. Marvelous. A lot of new clothes, I see. I wasn't sure until the minute I saw you that your folks would let you come. They must be really down on me for leaving the way I did. What's all this stuff you're carrying?" He picked up the packages and started to lead her out of the station.

"First," she said, "your plaque. Next,

apples for you, and a pie and Brown Betty for your mother."

"How thoughtful," he said. "Thank your mother for me."

He stepped forward and with Kathy following, he led her up the escalator to the front of the Port Authority building where a long black Cadillac, driven by a chauffeur, was waiting for them. The chauffeur stepped out, opened the door for them, then shut it as they sank back into the seats.

"Is this your car and chauffeur?" Kathy asked in an awed voice.

"My mother's," he grimaced. "That doesn't necessarily mean they're mine."

The car began to move and Chris put his arms around her, drew her to him, and then was kissing her as he had so many months ago, when their love seemed to be blossoming.

"No," she said, pushing him away.

"I know," he said. "You're angry because of my leaving. I don't blame you."

"Not angry," she said stiffly, "just wary. I don't want to start to like you again, Chris, until I understand why you acted the way you did. I don't want to be hurt again. I want some explanations."

"All right," he said quietly. "I'll explain everything to you after brunch." He sat back in his own corner of the car and said nothing. Then he reached out and took her hand, which he held tightly until they had stopped. She did not pull away.

"I don't feel any scars," she said.

"I'm lucky that my hands healed so well," he answered.

The car stopped in front of a tall apartment house, the chauffeur held the car door for them, and they walked into an elegant lobby, filled with mirrors and glittering, crystal chandeliers. "Good morning, Mr. Landers," the doorman said. "Good morning, Mr. Landers," the elevator operator said. "Good morning, miss."

It was almost impossible to connect this young, respected Mr. Landers with the ragged hitchhiker she had first known as Chris. It was also difficult to believe that this elegant young man had really been as enthusiastic as he had seemed to be about her mother's cooking, about apples, about agriculture. Nothing had ever been true, she thought with a sinking heart. It had all been a big act, right from the very first day when she had first suspected his sincerity. All along Chris had been playing a game. It reminded her of something she had learned in social studies: that the French aristocrats before the Revolution used to pretend to be shepherds and shepherdesses. She wished that she could flee at that moment. Chris would have nothing to explain to her. He had been playing a game, had unexpectedly hurt himself while playing, and then had taken off. It was all completely simple to her.

He rang the bell to his apartment and a uniformed maid opened the door for them.

"Good morning, sir," she said, "Good morning, miss."

Kathy stood in the foyer doorway and gasped at the magnificence within. Chris's home looked like a museum. The dining room alone was as large as the first floor of her house, and one entire wall of the apartment was made of glass and looked out on Central Park. Never before had she felt so poor, never before so ashamed of being poor.

Just then, a tall, blonde woman, dressed in what seemed to Kathy to be a chiffon evening gown (later she found out that it was a caftan robe), came bustling out to them. She was as made up and perfumed as if she were going out to the theater or a party, and she wore long, unmistakeably false eyelashes. Since her mother never used much makeup and disapproved of Kathy's use of anything more than lipstick, Kathy found herself so fascinated that she was guilty for a few minutes of staring. Nobody would ever dream that this woman was twenty years older than Mrs. Wright.

"How do you do," she said, holding out a white, manicured hand to Kathy. Kathy was mesmerized by the rings and long, perfect nails. Her voice was lazy and insolent and very much like her son's.

"I brought you some presents," Kathy said. "Apples, a pie, and a Brown Betty."

"Oh, thank you," she said. "Give them to Cora. She'll take them into the kitchen." She strode forward to the dining room and Kathy and Chris followed.

"We could have eaten in the breakfast room," Chris's mother said, "but Chris wanted you to enjoy the view of the park."

Only three places were set at the long table. Chris's mother sat at one end, Chris at the other, and Kathy was seated in between at the side. There were unusual shell mats under exquisite china, beautiful cut glasses for water, which felt heavier than she expected when she picked hers up, and snowy white, cloth napkins. A maid came around with a tray bearing freshly squeezed orange juice, a cut glass bowl of fresh raspberries and heavy cream, which Chris told her was called "clotted." Then Cora came in with hot, fragrant coffee, and rolls called croissants and brioches. The apricot jam had large pieces of apricots and was the best she had ever tasted.

She blushed with embarrassment, remembering how Chris had raved about her mother's cooking. How could he possibly have felt that way when he lived like this? Remembering their cluttered, old-fashioned kitchen, and seeing, in her mind, her mother wearing old jeans and bending over the stove, she was filled with shame and pity for her mother who had always worked so hard and looked so ordinary in contrast to the beautiful woman sitting as if carved in ice, at the end of the table.

"How was your trip?" Chris's mother asked in her throaty voice.

"Fine," Kathy said, unable to look directly at her.

"It was quite kind of your family to take my naughty son in this past summer," she said.

Kathy looked at her food, not knowing what to say. She remembered how intolerant she had been of Chuck's inarticulateness and now she was in exactly the same position. She felt particularly bad because she wanted to make a good impression for Chris.

The maid came in again. "Would you prefer a mushroom omelette or eggs Benedict, miss?" the maid asked. "Eggs Benedict," Kathy said, trying to sound as if she knew what they were. This was perhaps her only opportunity to find out.

The three of them sat there for a few more minutes while Chris's mother sipped her coffee from a tiny half-sized cup and smoked a cigarette. There seemed to be nothing more to say.

"If you'll excuse me now," she said, "my masseuse is coming."

Chris stood up and held his mother's chair. "Nice to have met you, Kathy," she said, and floated out of the room. Kathy had not the slightest idea of what a masseuse was.

"Your mother is very pretty," she told Chris.

"She should be," he said. "She's had her face lifted twice."

"Oh. Her nails are nice, too."

"Also fake," Chris grinned. Kathy wondered if he were telling her the truth.

The maid brought in the eggs Benedict. They were only poached eggs on English muffins with a cream sauce over them. "Please ring if you wish anything else, Mr. Chris," she said.

"Your mother didn't like me," she said to Chris.

"My mother doesn't like anyone who can't do something for her. You can't, ergo, you don't exist."

"She didn't like the gifts either," Kathy said. "I'm sorry I brought them."

"I like them," Chris said, "and I love your mother. Please thank her for me."

"Are you back at the same school you used to go to?" Kathy asked.

"Yes," he said, "but that was no easy matter. My mother had to make quite a big contribution to the Endowment Fund and I had to have a tutor every afternoon until I caught up."

"Did you catch up?"

"Yes."

"Chris," she said, finally pushing away her plate, "I want you to tell me why you took off that way without telling us. If you aren't going to tell me that now, I want to go home. I don't like it here."

"I don't blame you," he said. "I hate it myself. I told you that long ago."

"I didn't believe you about that then and I certainly don't believe you now. I think you always were lying to us, making fun of us, mocking us because we were country people."

"Please," he said. "Come with me to the den. It's too early for the museums. I promise that I'll tell you what you want to know when we're alone."

Grudgingly, she followed him down paneled hallways to a room that was all browns and beiges, with built-in furniture, bookcases, a complex stereo system, and soft couches around a fireplace in which a small cannel coal fire blazed. He added some coal, then sank down beside her on one of the couches.

"Well," she said.

"All right. Kathy, did you ever wonder why I left the plaque?"

"It probably couldn't fit into your knapsack."

"Oh, Kathy," he said. "Of course that wasn't why." To her surprise, there were tears in his eyes. "I left it because I was responsible for the fire."

"You, responsible? That's ridiculous, Chris. You were the hero, not the cause."

"I was the cause," he said. "I had been working with the pickers since early morning, and you know how obsessed your father is with cigarettes. But I was tired and bored and a little restless and I wanted one. I just felt I had to have a cigarette and I resented anybody's interference with what I do to my own body. So I went around to the door of the warehouse, walked inside so nobody would see me, and lit a cigarette. I finished the cigarette and tossed the butt away without thinking. Then I closed my eyes and dozed off for about five minutes. When I opened them, the fire had started and was spreading like nothing I'd ever seen. Even while I stood there and watched, new things kept catching. I didn't know what to do. So I ran to your house and your mother called the fire department. Then I dashed back down to the warehouse and stood there feeling suicidal. I didn't know what to do.

"In less than five minutes, the firemen were there and then suddenly I remembered the gas storage tank. Your father was there by then and he asked the firemen to get it out, but they didn't think they could. So I went inside and started to pull on it. There was no time to get gloves, that's why my hands were burned. I pulled the tank out just in time for your dad and the firemen to see me and call me a 'hero.'"

Kathy moved closer to him and held his hand while he finished telling her his terrible story.

"You can't imagine how awful I felt, Kathy. All that week when I was lying there in front of the television, I wanted to die. I was sorry I hadn't died in the fire. Your family was better to me than any people I had ever known before, better to me than my own mother, and I had ruined things for you. I felt like such a fraud. I wanted to confess to you, to anyone, but I just didn't know how to do it. Also, I was afraid that if the insurance company found out about it, that might interfere with your father's getting the insurance money. I was even afraid of going to jail. I thought maybe you could go to jail for setting a fire, even if it was accidental. I was an arsonist.

"I kept thinking night and day about what to do, Kathy. I couldn't sleep when I wasn't drugged. I felt like a robot. You can't imagine the guilt. I would have left the day after the fire but I didn't feel well enough to hitch. Then there was that party. I had no idea that they were going to give me that plaque and that made me feel worse than ever. That's why I left it.

"I figured that the only thing to do would be to come back here and get some money from my mother. I intended to write all of this to you and enclose a check with it. But my mother flatly refused. She said I would just have to wait until I came into some money myself, when I turn eighteen and get small trusts from my father and grandmother. I pleaded with her, but she said insurance would take care of things and that if the place was such a tinderbox anyway, she refused to accept my responsibility for the fire. She said that if I persisted in looking for things to feel guilty about, I should see a psychiatrist.

"So I went back to school and started to talk to the guidance counselor there. After a while, he was able to convince me to write to you, even though I won't have the money for a few months. Well, that's the story, Kathy. Do you think that you or your family can ever forgive me?"

Tears were running down his face. With a cry of love she threw her arms around him and cried with him, her face against his, their tears mingling. She held him tightly until they'd both stopped crying. "Come on," he said, "I'll show you my New York."

They walked along Fifth Avenue, enjoying the brisk fall day. At the Metropolitan Museum they visited the Egyptian collection and the exhibit of Russian clothes. Kathy was fascinated with how tiny the Empress Catherine's waist had been at the time of her marriage and how much bigger her costumes were later on. Before they left, Chris took her to the cafeteria beside the onyx pool and ordered cappuccinos for them, wonderful, steamed coffee and foamy milk with cinnamon on top. It was a little bitter without sugar, but with one teaspoon, it became delicious.

They held on to each other tightly, their happiness marred by fear and uncertainty about the future. "And now," Chris said, "it's time for Radio City." It was the most beautiful movie theater Kathy had ever seen, probably the most beautiful in the whole world, and she loved every minute of the time there, especially watching the Rockettes. Dusk was falling when they walked back to his apartment. The maid let them in. Chris's mother was talking to someone on the library phone. The door was open and her caustic voice carried to them perfectly.

"You would not believe," Kathy heard her say, "the perfectly dreadful farm girl Chris brought home with him today. A vinyl purse, the most tacky clothes; probably all ordered from the Sears catalogue or wherever it is people like that get their clothing. She brought me a gift of Apple Brown Betty.

"Well, you know how difficult Chris is. He's always insisted on being a little weird, rebellious, going out of his way to spite me. With all of the lovely girls at his school and at the club, he went out of his way to dig this one up. The girl knows nothing, absolutely nothing. Talk about a *tabula rasa.* He found one. It's like bringing home one of the Beverly Hillbillies, but at least they had money."

Kathy looked at Chris, stricken, her eyes filled with tears. The pleasures of the last few hours were instantly swept away. Furious, Chris walked to the library, reached inside for the door, and slammed it shut with all his strength. Then he took Kathy's hand and, like a little child, she docilely followed him to the den. Shaking with humiliation, she sat on the couch. "I want to leave right now," she told Chris. "I want to try to make an earlier bus. I'll call my dad after I check the schedule."

"Just give me five minutes," he said. He put an old Marx Brothers movie on to cheer her up, then walked out to talk to his mother. He came back into the room a few minutes later, still angry, looking like the old Chris, wearing jeans, a pea jacket, and cowboy boots. He was holding his old knapsack.

"I told her I was going," he said. "Call your father. Please tell him that I want to come back with you, that is if I'm still welcome."

"Are you sure about this?" she asked. "Do you really know what you're doing?"

"Yes, I'm sure," he said.

She dialed and got her father almost immediately. Then she told him that she would be making an earlier bus and that Chris wanted to come with her.

"I don't know," her father said. "Do you really want this, Kathy?"

"Please, Dad."

"All right," he said, "if this is what you want. We'll leave some dinner for the two of you."

"I don't want to take my mother's car," Chris said, ignoring the waiting limousine parked at the curb. He asked the doorman to hail a cab, which they took to the Port Authority. After Chris had purchased his ticket they sat in the restaurant, drinking coffee and waiting for the bus.

"I really want to apologize for what my mother said," he told Kathy. "Nobody with a heart would ever want to hurt you."

"She can't hurt me," Kathy said bravely, "as long as *you* love me."

"I love you," he said, "and I'm never going to leave you again."

EPILOGUE

They sat on the bus together, his arm around her, close and loving and connected.

"This is going to be the hardest thing I've ever done," he said.

"Not as hard, I think," Kathy answered, "as what you've been through. I think telling him will make you feel better."

When the bus pulled into their station, Kathy could see her father waiting patiently outside.

"Look how clear the night is, Chris," she caroled joyously. "You can see the stars up here." The moon was full and the air was crisp and renewing.

"And you can breathe here, too," Chris answered.

"Hello, sir," Chris said, gravely shaking her father's hand. "Thank you for letting me come. I want to explain to you . . ."

"Later," Mr. Wright said. "Now let's go home. Mother kept dinner warm for the two of you."

Stephan was waiting in the car, and he jumped up and down in pleasure when he saw Chris. "Are you going to stay with us for good now?" he asked.

"If your folks will let me stay," Chris said.

"Hey, Chris, in class we were reading a book about superstitions, and do you know there are a lot of superstitions about apples? Listen to this one, 'If you can eat a crab apple without frowning, you can get the person you desire.' "

"I'll have to try that," Chris said, smiling at Kathy.

"Here's another one," Stephan said, " 'If you can break an apple in two, you can get anyone you choose as your life partner.' "

"I'd like to try that one, too," Chris laughed.

When they reached the house, Kathy stood outside for a moment to look at her mother through the window. There she stood, as always, working at the stove. Her hair was pulled back in a bun, and escaping pieces curled around her head. She wore no makeup and she looked comfortable, but not young or pretty like Chris's mother. Kathy's heart was pierced so sharply with love that she ran inside to hold her mother in her arms.

Her mother kissed her and let out a little

cry of pleasure when she saw Chris. "I was so pleased when I heard that Kathy was bringing you back. How wonderful. Are you here to stay?" She ran over to Chris and gave him a hug and kiss.

"If you still want me," Chris said unsmilingly. "I have to talk to you both."

"Eat first," Mrs. Wright said, "then we'll talk over coffee."

The cloth on the table was old, some of the screens had holes in them, the linoleum was almost rubbed thin in places, and Mrs. Wright was perspiring slightly as she worked at the stove. Their dishes were old Corning Ware, and their napkins were paper. Mrs. Wright sliced the still warm ham for them, dished out succotash and mashed potatoes, passed the cold, homemade red cabbage, and then joined them at the table as they ate. Finally they were through. Kathy poured coffee for them all, Stephan took another glass of cider, and her parents looked expectantly at Chris. Without asking for pity, without excusing himself, he told them the truth of the fire. When he had finished, he looked at them timidly, ready to take flight.

"You poor boy," Mrs. Wright said. "What a terrible thing to live with for so long." She walked over to him, put her arms around him and kissed him.

"Will you trust me to repay you when I

am eighteen and get my money?" Chris asked Mr. Wright.

"Yes," said Mr. Wright, "if we still need it. We'll discuss it further then. But if you want to stay with us, Chris, there must be some changes. You can't stay out there over the garage. It's too cold. You'll have to move in with Stephan."

"Yippee," Stephan sang.

"And you'll have to go to school with Kathy," Mr. Wright continued. "Will you do that?"

"Yes," Chris said, "if that's what you'd like me to do."

"And, Chris," Mr. Wright added, "I would appreciate it if you didn't tell anyone outside of this family the truth of the fire. It will be a lot easier for you to adjust to this community, and for them to adjust to you, if the other kids continue to think of you as a hero."

"Thank you," Chris said simply.

"Hey, Kathy," Stephan broke into her reverie. "What do you want for Christmas? Huh?"

"What do I want for Christmas?" she echoed. She looked around the room. "What do I want for Christmas?" she repeated. "I want just what I have right now. That's what I want."

Stephan got out the Scrabble board and they sat on the floor playing until *Saturday*

Night Live came on. Kathy felt a deeper contentment than she had ever before known. She was lucky. Lucky in her parents, in Stephan, and in Chris; lucky that Chris had decided to come back. She didn't know what the future held for them. Maybe they would continue to always love each other as her parents had done, but maybe they would grow apart when they went to college. Maybe they could both go to the same college. Maybe they would spend their lives working with apples. Somewhere she had once read: "Man's character is his destiny." She looked up from the game at the faces of her parents. Their characters were also the destiny of their children. She didn't know what lay ahead. But she was sure that whatever came, it would be good and right for them all.

cry of pleasure when she saw Chris. "I was so pleased when I heard that Kathy was bringing you back. How wonderful. Are you here to stay?" She ran over to Chris and gave him a hug and kiss.

"If you still want me," Chris said unsmilingly. "I have to talk to you both."

"Eat first," Mrs. Wright said, "then we'll talk over coffee."

The cloth on the table was old, some of the screens had holes in them, the linoleum was almost rubbed thin in places, and Mrs. Wright was perspiring slightly as she worked at the stove. Their dishes were old Corning Ware, and their napkins were paper. Mrs. Wright sliced the still warm ham for them, dished out succotash and mashed potatoes, passed the cold, homemade red cabbage, and then joined them at the table as they ate. Finally they were through. Kathy poured coffee for them all, Stephan took another glass of cider, and her parents looked expectantly at Chris. Without asking for pity, without excusing himself, he told them the truth of the fire. When he had finished, he looked at them timidly, ready to take flight.

"You poor boy," Mrs. Wright said. "What a terrible thing to live with for so long." She walked over to him, put her arms around him and kissed him.

"Will you trust me to repay you when I

am eighteen and get my money?" Chris
asked Mr. Wright.

"Yes," said Mr. Wright, "if we still need
it. We'll discuss it further then. But if you
want to stay with us, Chris, there must be
some changes. You can't stay out there over
the garage. It's too cold. You'll have to move
in with Stephan."

"Yippee," Stephan sang.

"And you'll have to go to school with
Kathy," Mr. Wright continued. "Will you do
that?"

"Yes," Chris said, "if that's what you'd
like me to do."

"And, Chris," Mr. Wright added, "I would
appreciate it if you didn't tell anyone outside
of this family the truth of the fire. It will be
a lot easier for you to adjust to this community, and for them to adjust to you, if the
other kids continue to think of you as a
hero."

"Thank you," Chris said simply.

"Hey, Kathy," Stephan broke into her
reverie. "What do you want for Christmas?
Huh?"

"What do I want for Christmas?" she
echoed. She looked around the room. "What
do I want for Christmas?" she repeated.
"I want just what I have right now. That's
what I want."

Stephan got out the Scrabble board and
they sat on the floor playing until *Saturday*

Night Live came on. Kathy felt a deeper contentment than she had ever before known. She was lucky. Lucky in her parents, in Stephan, and in Chris; lucky that Chris had decided to come back. She didn't know what the future held for them. Maybe they would continue to always love each other as her parents had done, but maybe they would grow apart when they went to college. Maybe they could both go to the same college. Maybe they would spend their lives working with apples. Somewhere she had once read: "Man's character is his destiny." She looked up from the game at the faces of her parents. Their characters were also the destiny of their children. She didn't know what lay ahead. But she was sure that whatever came, it would be good and right for them all.